# Norah
## Brides of Fremont County, Book 4
## by Cat Cahill

D1706275

# Copyright

# Chapter One

*CAÑON CITY, COLORADO — September 1882*

Norah Parker nearly stepped on the gift this time.

The little parcel—wrapped in plain brown paper with string—had been left on the first step just below the porch.

"Oh!" Norah hopped sideways over it, grabbing hold of the wrought iron handrail to keep from losing her balance.

The door flew open, and Norah's mother stepped outside. "Are you all right?" she asked.

"I believe so." Norah placed a hand to her chest. "Someone has left a package on the steps."

"That's curious." Mama retrieved the parcel, examined it, and held it out to Norah. "It bears your name."

Norah took one look at the handwriting on the paper and sighed. It was from Mr. Beck.

*Again.*

She slipped the string off and gently tore open the paper, wondering what sort of everyday item he'd sent her this time. His past gifts had included a chicken, a collection of previously used glass jars, and a broom, and so many other items over the past year and a half—none of which Norah could ever imagine a man choosing for a lady he wished to court.

This time, she extracted a pair of spectacles.

1

"Mr. Beck?" Mama said, trying and failing to hold back a smile.

"Who else?" Norah bit her lip, but giggles escaped despite her best efforts as she held out the "gift" to her mother.

Mama held up the spectacles and shook her head. "He's a dear old man. Did you speak with him again?"

"Yes, and I'd hoped that seven times might be enough. But apparently he's not easily dissuaded." Mr. Beck was older than her father—and for reasons unknown to Norah—was entirely taken with her.

"At this point, I believe only your marriage to someone else will convince him to end his pursuit."

"I don't know. He'd likely continue, hoping to be first in line in the event I'm widowed."

Mama laughed. "Go on. Give Ruthann my love. I'll see if your father can't make use of these spectacles."

Norah gave her a grateful smile and hurried down the stairs. The dull gifts from Mr. Beck *did* bring a smile to her face, even as she wished the man would turn his attention to the widowed ladies of his own age. After all, it wasn't as if any other man was paying her any attentions. Of course, it might help if she wasn't so preoccupied at social occasions that she could speak more than two words to potential suitors.

Thoughts of beaux flitted quickly from her mind as she walked the short distance to Harper's Photographic Studio, where her dearest friend, Ruthann Harper, lived in the rooms above the studio with her new husband. Ruthann was the only person who understood what consumed Norah's mind most of the time. She was the only one with whom Norah felt as if she didn't need to affix a smile to her face and speak of banal topics like hats and weather. Even as Norah suspected her parents and her eldest brother Charles went around pretending most of the time too, she didn't dare speak of her brother Jeremy to them. Not after they'd made it clear he was no longer part of their family.

But Norah couldn't forget so easily. Particularly when she didn't believe most of what people said about Jeremy—that judge included.

And after over two years of worrying and wondering, it was high time she spoke with him herself to find out the truth.

Inside the studio, she greeted Nate, Ruthann's husband and one of Jeremy's closest childhood friends. He was arranging some of his equipment, so Norah hurried along to the second floor. As she climbed the stairs, she wondered what Nate's thoughts were about her brother. Ruthann had told her that Nate asked about him once and had indicated that he'd like to see Jeremy, but hadn't mentioned it since.

Did he know what Ruthann had planned for today?

At the top of the steps, Norah adjusted her hat, smoothed down her skirts, and knocked. The door opened to reveal Norah's dearest friend. Ruthann gave her a broad smile and stepped back to allow her to come inside.

"Norah is here," she called softly over her shoulder, most likely as to not to wake baby Caleb. Turning back to Norah, she said—more for show than for information since Norah already knew of her plan, "I asked Stuart to come by and help me move some furniture. Nate's been so busy downstairs that I hate to take him away from his work. And Stuart's employer is so very understanding." Ruthann shot a smile at her brother, who had stood from his seat on the settee.

Norah stifled a giggle. Stuart's employer was their father, who ran one of the largest of the many shipping and freight businesses in town.

"I'll pass that compliment on to our father," he said to Ruthann before turning his gaze toward Norah. "It's good to see you, Norah."

An odd shiver traced its way down Norah's spine as he spoke. His blue eyes held hers, and for a moment, she wondered why he seemed so intrigued with her.

Until she realized he was waiting for a response.

"Yes," she blurted out finally, feeling completely ridiculous, just as Ruthann's expression began to change to one of concern. "It's nice to see you, too, Stuart. How is your work?"

"It's busy, but never too busy for my little sister, apparently," he said with a glance at Ruthann. "Thank you for asking, Norah."

Behind his back, Ruthann stuck out her tongue at him. Norah covered her mouth to hide her smile.

Stuart reached for his hat. "I ought to be—"

"Oh, no!" Ruthann sprang into action, taking the hat from his grasp and hanging it back up. "You can't go yet. Norah only just arrived! And the baby hasn't woken. Surely you'd like to see your nephew."

Stuart looked back and forth between them, a tiny wrinkle appearing between his eyebrows. "I thought you two might want to visit. And besides, Papa—"

"Oh, Papa will be just fine without you for a bit longer. Sit! I'll fetch us some tea." Ruthann bustled off to the kitchen, which was only steps away from the parlor in the small apartment.

Stuart narrowed his eyes slightly as he watched Ruthann set the kettle on the stove. His sky-colored gaze slid back to Norah. "Do you know what's going on here? I suspect Ruthann has something up her sleeve."

"I . . ." Norah looked to Ruthann for help. It had been Ruthann's idea, although Norah was more than happy to go along with it.

Ruthann gave her brother a petulant look. "Now, why would you think such a thing?"

Stuart crossed his arms. "Because I know you too well. I visit with my nephew frequently, and you've never once offered to make me tea when I've come by here."

Ruthann sighed. "I'd like to ask a favor of you. For Norah."

Stuart glanced at Norah, looking for all the world as if he couldn't imagine what she might need from him. She gave him a smile, hoping it belied the utter lack of courage she felt at the moment.

"You could have been direct," he said to Ruthann. "I'm always happy to help a friend. What is it you need assistance with?" Stuart held her gaze again, and all the words flew out of Norah's head.

She'd known Stuart all her life, had seen him daily in school when they were young, and when visiting Ruthann at their family home. She remembered that awkward time when his hair wouldn't lie flat and the occasion when he'd stolen her schoolbooks and hidden them in the privy. Yet after all of that, she couldn't ask him the most important question she'd ever had.

Thankfully, Ruthann stepped in. Leaving the kettle to heat on the stove, she came back into the parlor and took Norah's hand in hers.

Stuart looked particularly curious now, that wrinkle between his eyebrows growing even deeper. "Do you have an overly persistent suitor? I'm more than happy to run him off."

Ruthann smirked as she held fast to Norah's hand. "We all know how good you are at such things." He'd disapproved of every gentleman interested in Ruthann before her marriage.

Just as Norah thought she might ask him to help her dissuade Mr. Beck instead of speaking about the real reason she needed his assistance, Ruthann plunged ahead with their request.

"It isn't a suitor. It's Jeremy. Norah has made up her mind to pay him a visit, but she can't go alone. Will you accompany her?"

He was going to say no. It was evident in the way his expression changed from one of surprise to one that could have been made from stone.

"Absolutely not," he said.

And that was it. Her only chance at learning how to prove her brother's innocence had been discarded in the space of two words. Norah's heart sank.

She would never know the truth now.

# Chapter Two

STUART CLENCHED HIS jaw. How could Ruthann ask such a thing of him? Jeremy might have been his friend once, but that ended the moment he refused to step away from trouble. And that trouble landed him in the place he deserved to be—the Territorial Prison at the edge of town.

"Are your parents aware of your plans?" He posed the question to Norah, knowing already what the answer would be.

"Of course not," she said. When she looked up at him, her eyes—a fascinating shade of blue flecked with brown—were watery.

She was about to cry, and it was because of him.

He distracted himself from the guilt rising from his gut by looking at his sister. Ruthann had her chin lifted defiantly, and he knew he was about to hear every thought that had just gone through her head.

"Stuart Joliet. I know you're angry at him and you have every right to be. But Norah's done nothing wrong. Her family might have cut ties with Jeremy, but her heart has been heavy for so long now. Haven't you noticed?"

He'd noticed. Always soft-spoken, though not shy, Norah had gone even more quiet. She'd attended social events, but had spoken only to those she knew best. And every time she smiled, it appeared as if it were a ghost of the smiles that had come before.

It hurt to see a girl so full of life turn into a quiet shadow. But Jeremy's actions had hurt them all. Stuart would never forget that. Paying his former friend a visit would mean he accepted the choices Jeremy had made.

"You'd be better off forgetting him," he said to Norah in a low voice.

Her unshed tears disappeared in an instant. "I won't. He's my brother, and I *know* he did nothing wrong. I'll never forget him, and I'll *never* stop missing him." Her words were like fire, matching the anger that had flared up in those fascinating eyes.

Her response was so unexpected that Stuart nearly took a step backward. Gathering himself, he thought that perhaps she would listen to reason instead.

"The evidence presented against him was irrefutable," he said. And indeed, it had been. When Jeremy's former employer, along with several other men of standing in the town, all testified to Jeremy's change in habits, friends, and motivation to rob a train that sat overnight at the depot, there was no room left for doubt.

"I don't care," Norah said with a quiet intensity. Her fists were clenched now, Ruthann's hand wrapped around her arm. "Jeremy would never steal, and he *certainly* would never murder anyone in order to steal." She paused. "I know him. And I thought you did too."

Her words were a knife to the chest, twisting through his heart. His resolve faltered for a moment. What harm could it cause, paying Jeremy a visit? He wouldn't even have to say anything. He would only need accompany Norah and let her do the talking.

And if her father found out . . .

"No." It came out more forcefully than Stuart meant it. Softening his words, he added, "Ruthann's told me your parents have forbidden you from contacting him. I couldn't disobey them like that, even if I wanted to. I have too much respect for your father."

"How funny," Ruthann said. "I seem to recall you not caring at all what *our* father said about riding up into the hills a few years ago. Where was your so-called respect to your own father? And what about that time he expressly forbade you to visit that old, dingy saloon—"

"All right." He glared at his sister. How did she always know the precise way to sway an argument?

"All I'm saying is that your nobility as far as parents are concerned has a dubious history."

Could she make him sound like less of a gentleman?

"My parents would never find out—not about my visit, and certainly not that you accompanied me," Norah said. The anger had dimmed from her eyes, replaced now by an almost pleading look. It seared through his soul, making him feel as if he were a terrible sort of person for not agreeing to the one thing that could lift her spirits. She brushed a lock of her red-brown hair behind her ear, and Stuart knew right then and there that he couldn't refuse her.

She'd been hurting for far too long, and he hated seeing any woman in pain, much less an old friend of his sister's. If seeing Jeremy would make Norah genuinely smile again, he'd ignore his own opinions on the matter and take the risk.

"Fine," he said, barely gritting out the word. "I'll do it. But I have nothing to say to him myself."

Ruthann grinned at Norah and then flung her arms around Stuart. "I knew you'd agree! Thank you!"

"Thank you, Stuart," Norah echoed when Ruthann stepped back. The look in her eyes conveyed more than words ever could.

Stuart tugged at his vest, acting as if Ruthann's embrace had rumpled it. He wasn't certain when he'd last felt so embarrassed by someone's gratitude before, but Norah's had him feeling as if he needed to unbutton his collar to breathe.

"It's fine," he said, his words mumbled.

"Will you go soon?" Ruthann asked as she ran to fetch the boiling kettle.

"As soon as Norah wishes to go," he answered.

"Perhaps the day after tomorrow?" Norah's gaze was unfocused, as if her mind were at work. Likely trying to come up with what she'd tell her parents, he thought. He tried not to cringe at the idea of going along with her deception. He had nothing but respect for Mr. and Mrs. Parker, and they'd always treated him as another son.

"Yes, that's fine. Shall I fetch you at home?"

"No . . ." Norah shook her head as she appeared to think. "May we meet here, Ruthann? To avoid any awkward explanation if Mama or Papa is at home?"

"Certainly," Ruthann said as she poured a cup of tea for each of them.

He'd need to excuse himself from his work yet again, but there was no getting around it. "I'll meet you here at three o'clock."

Norah nodded her assent as baby Caleb sent up a cry from the bedroom. Ruthann gestured for them to sit in the kitchen as she rushed to fetch her son. When she returned with the baby, the girls continued to talk, but Stuart drank the hot tea as quickly as he dared. He needed to get outside, draw in some fresh air, and think.

On the excuse that he really did need to return to work, he bid Ruthann and Norah farewell and hurried down the stairs. Thankfully, Nate was hidden away in the darkroom he used to turn the images he took with his camera into photographs. Stuart didn't know what he'd say to his friend about what he'd just agreed to.

In fact, he didn't know Nate's thoughts at all about Jeremy. They'd avoided the topic in conversation, much to Stuart's relief. It was easier not to think about Jeremy than it was to talk about him.

Outside, the street bustled with people on their way to and from shops, offices, and homes. Stuart smiled at several friendly faces and greeted a handful of people, but quickly veered off onto a side street. He needed to be alone for a moment. To run the past hour through his head and get his thoughts straight.

He found himself walking among homes. There were a few people about, but not nearly as many as there were in the center of town. And his mind began to wander.

Ruthann and Norah's request had taken him by surprise, but really, it shouldn't have at all. Given Norah's subdued nature since Jeremy went to prison, he ought to have known she was planning something like this all along. She was a devoted sister, loyal and kind, and she'd proven that many times over the years. He'd never forget finding himself with a clod of dirt striking his back, and then turning around to find a defiant No-rah had been the one who'd thrown it. All because he'd pushed Jeremy into the river.

"You could have killed him!" Stuart remembered her say-ing, dirt-stained hands on her hips.

"It was hardly running," had been his reply. And although it had been true—the river was a shallow, slow thing in August, and he would have never truly endangered his friend—he couldn't have helped but feel ashamed at her accusation.

Of course she wanted to see Jeremy now. And of course she believed he was innocent of all the charges that had been levied against him.

Although he hated helping her deceive her parents, he couldn't help but admire her audacity. He would help her visit her brother—and then he'd have to be there when Jeremy dis-appointed her. When she finally came to the conclusion the rest of them already had—Jeremy was guilty.

It had been the hardest thing Stuart had to make peace with in his life, but he hadn't lied to himself. His friend was no longer the man he'd known or the boy he'd grown up with. He'd turned into someone else entirely.

It was best to bury the past in order to move toward the fu-ture.

# Chapter Three

THE HIGH STONE WALL surrounding the Colorado State Penitentiary—which everyone in Cañon City still referred to as the Territorial Prison—was so imposing that part of Norah simply wanted to turn around and return home.

But Stuart was at her side, her arm tucked around his in a gentlemanly manner, and his presence gave her courage. He didn't want to be here, yet she and Ruthann had talked him into it. She wouldn't waste his time with cowardice.

Besides, seeing Jeremy was worth a few moments of fear.

Thankfully, Stuart did the talking for her as they approached the guards. They were let inside, and he paid the fee required before Norah could fumble for the funds in her reticule. After being informed they could not return again for three months, they were led to a room empty of everything except a table and two chairs.

"Are you all right?" Stuart asked as soon as the door closed behind the guard who had gone to fetch Jeremy.

"Yes," she replied, clasping her hands together to keep them from trembling.

Stuart pulled out one of the chairs at the table, gesturing for her to sit. Norah gratefully sank into it. "It is an intimidating place, isn't it?" he mused.

Norah nodded. Her worries were now more related to Jeremy than to the prison itself. How did he survive here? It had been so long—what would he look like when she saw him? What if he didn't want to see her?

Her throat clenched at the last thought. To distract herself, she looked up at Stuart, who stood beside her with his arms crossed, facing the door.

"Do you suppose they're fed well here?" she asked.

"I presume so. They keep hogs, and every time I've seen the men working outside these walls, they didn't appear to be starving."

Well, that was at least one less thing to worry about.

The minutes ticked by. What was taking so long? Norah twisted her hands together, over and over, as if the motion would ensure Jeremy's prompt arrival.

A large hand covered hers, pressing gently.

Her hands stilled instantly. The warmth of Stuart's palm, even through her gloves, was comforting. The second he pulled his hand away, she wished he hadn't.

"He'll want to see you," he said. "If you're worried that he won't."

Norah looked up at him in surprise. How had he known exactly what she was thinking? "What if he's angry with me for not writing or visiting before this?"

Stuart shook his head. He squatted down until he was eye-level with her. "He won't be. If he has a shred of decency left, he'll have understood your position."

Stuart spoke with such assurance that Norah nodded. His eyes held hers, and she was reminded of the way she'd lost her ability to speak two days ago when he'd looked at her so intently. She couldn't have spoken now either, but the way he looked at her made her feel as if everything would work out as it should.

The door creaked open, and Stuart stood quickly. He stepped forward, not directly in front of Norah, but just far enough to be protective. She barely registered his actions before her gaze caught Jeremy.

He was leaner than he'd been two years ago, but in a way that indicated he was working harder than he had when he'd held his job at the railroad depot. He wore the striped clothing of a prisoner, and his light brown hair was more neatly trimmed than it had ever been. But his eyes . . .

It took everything inside of Norah not to gasp and cover her mouth. Instead, she pressed her hands against her knees as her brother's sad, empty eyes began to fill with a light she doubted they'd had since he'd arrived here.

A smile grew across his face as the guard indicated he should sit in the chair opposite Norah. It was as if her very presence gave him a reason to go on living.

As Stuart spoke briefly with the guard, Norah returned Jeremy's smile. But her heart ached with the action. How long had he waited for someone to come visit with him only to be disappointed every day?

Any guilt she had about deceiving her parents vanished. Jeremy needed this, and Norah wished she'd come sooner.

"You don't know how good it does me to see you both," Jeremy said in a choked voice the second the guard stepped back to the corner and Stuart returned to stand near Norah.

Norah wanted so badly to stand and embrace her brother, but not knowing precisely what was allowed, she forced herself to remain seated. "I'm sorry I didn't come sooner. I wish I had." She paused. "Our parents don't know I'm here."

Jeremy winced slightly, and whether it was because she'd broken the rules to visit him or because he now knew Mama and Papa hadn't allowed it, she didn't know. He glanced up at Stuart. "Thank you for bringing her."

Stuart said nothing. He stood like that wall of stone outside—tall, arms crossed, impenetrable expression. Norah bit her lip and wished he'd say something, even if it wasn't kind.

Finally, he inclined his head slightly in answer to Jeremy's gratitude. Jeremy studied him a moment before turning back to Norah.

"How is everyone at home?"

"They're all well. Charles and Mary are expecting a baby early next year."

Jeremy grinned at the news of their older brother becoming a father.

"Are you all right here?" Norah asked, resting her hands on the table and leaning forward. "Do they treat you well? I've worried so much about you."

"I get enough to eat. Working in the quarry makes the days pass more quickly." His voice was subdued, and Norah's heart clenched. He'd been so proud of his job at the depot, where he'd engaged with railroad passengers and businesses needing to ship freight all over the country. He would have become stationmaster in a few years when Mr. Rose stepped down. And now he spent his days chipping away at rock.

Norah looked down at her hands, encased in a pair of new white gloves. She had everything she needed and the freedom to go where she chose, within reason.

Jeremy used to have all of that too. He wouldn't have given it all up willingly. She'd been certain of that when he was first arrested, and she'd grown even more certain over the passage of time.

She looked up and met Jeremy's eyes. "Will you tell me what happened? I heard you didn't even defend yourself at the trial."

Stuart shifted next to her, but he remained silent. He wanted to know too, Norah was almost certain. She knew he hadn't been in attendance at the trial either. He might believe Jeremy was guilty, but he wanted to hear the words from him.

Jeremy sat back, his shoulders drooping. He glanced at the guard near the door as if trying to determine whether to speak in front of him. "I did nothing wrong," he finally said in a low voice.

She waited for him to say more, but he didn't. She leaned forward again, lowering her voice. "I don't understand. And I don't believe you're capable of . . . of *murdering* anyone, much less some innocent railroadman."

Jeremy wouldn't meet her eyes. "You're correct."

"And? You must give me more than that, Jeremy!" She needed to know the whole of the truth.

"That's all I can say." He finally looked up at her again. "It's enough for me to know you believe me. It will make the days here easier."

Norah wanted to leap up and slam her hands on the table. Irritation shot through her as she forced herself to remain seated. Coming here, all she'd wanted was the truth. But now, knowing that, she needed more. She wanted details, an explanation, all the information he could provide.

She wanted to help him. But how could she possibly do that if he wouldn't say more?

"Why can't you tell me anything else? I want to know what happened. Your family deserves to know the circumstances. Else how can we . . . How can I—"

A hand on her shoulder cut off her words. She looked up, startled, to find Stuart gazing back at her with an expression of wariness. He shook his head just ever so slightly, and Norah swallowed her words.

He removed his hand, taking back a comfortable weight that kept her tethered to reason. "We know enough," he said, his eyes now on Jeremy. "You abandoned your family and your true friends for false promises of wealth. You threw away a good life to take what you wanted. A man *died* because of your greed, Parker."

"Stuart!" Norah protested. His words were so cold. She thought he'd stopped her because he suspected there was some reason Jeremy wouldn't give them more of the truth. But he was letting his anger overcome his sense. If he could only re-member who Jeremy was, he'd know her brother was telling the truth. If he would only give Jeremy the benefit of the doubt, then perhaps they could learn more.

Perhaps they could *help* him.

Jeremy closed his eyes at Stuart's words, and Norah could only imagine how much they hurt him. But he said nothing to defend himself.

"It's true," Stuart said to Norah before looking back toward Jeremy. "She'd be much better off if you told her the truth rather than hiding behind lies of innocence." Although his voice was edged in ice, a current of sadness ran beneath it.

Norah hadn't noticed it before, but the way Stuart caught his breath after speaking, and the way he clenched his jaw as if he were forcing down emotion gave it away.

And it was no wonder. Jeremy had been his closest friend. And by all appearances, Jeremy had tossed aside that friendship with nary a glance behind him.

But this was a good sign. It meant Stuart *wanted* to believe Jeremy, despite everything he'd told himself.

"I spoke the truth to Norah. And to you," Jeremy said in a quiet voice. "And that's all I can say. I trust you'll understand."

"But I don't—" Norah started.

"Now I ought to get back." Jeremy gestured toward the guard, who began walking toward them. "I love you, Norah. I miss you and everyone else every day. If you're able to write, I have the privilege of sending and receiving letters."

Norah nodded, her throat tightening. There was so much more she wanted to know. So much Jeremy hadn't said. And now he was leaving, and she couldn't come back for three months—if she dared to defy her parents again. And if Stuart would acquiesce to accompany her a second time.

"Jeremy," she said, forcing his name past the lump in her throat. "I'll write."

He flashed her that smile she remembered so well. If her letters could make him smile like that, she'd write hundreds and hundreds of them.

"Wait here," the guard instructed before leaving with Jeremy.

The door shut behind her brother, and Norah swallowed hard. She knew two things for certain now.

First, Jeremy was most definitely innocent of the crimes for which he'd been imprisoned.

And second, it was up to her to find a way to help him. But she couldn't do it alone.

"Stuart." She whirled around to face him. "I need your help."

# Chapter Four

THAT FIRE WAS BACK in Norah's eyes. The one that had blazed when Stuart had originally declined to bring her here to visit Jeremy. It was the sort of look that would make it nearly impossible to say no to her.

But Stuart had the sneaking suspicion that what she was about to ask him was something he wanted no part of at all.

"Of course I'll help you if I can," he found himself saying despite every alarm sounding in his mind.

"We must prove Jeremy's innocence. You *know* he didn't commit those crimes. I know you're angry, and anger makes people say things they wish they hadn't. You want to believe him—I know you do." Her lips pressed together in determination and she watched him with an expression that almost dared him to say no to her.

He had to step around this very carefully. Under no circumstances did he want Norah running off to do this on her own if he disagreed. Yet he also didn't want to get her hopes up. It would be so much easier if she could simply believe the truth of the matter.

Jeremy wasn't the brother she'd known.

"That could prove to be very difficult," he said gently.

"And that's why I need your assistance." She crossed the bare room, reminding Stuart of himself when he was deep in thought. "You know so many more people than I do through your work. Surely between the two of us, we can discover some new piece of information—some sort of evidence—that will show Jeremy couldn't have possibly done what they've said."

Stuart set his jaw. She was quite determined. It was evident in the way she held herself, the hurried way she spoke, and the vibrant way she kept glancing at him. It was good to see Norah so lively again. He only wished it were for some other reason. "He's already been tried and convicted."

"Surely a judge will re-examine that verdict if we find out the truth!" She paused, halfway across the room, and tilted her head as she looked at him. "You do want to believe Jeremy, don't you?"

He took a deep breath. He wanted to. Badly. He had all along. But when the truth was right there in front of his face, it would be like believing in a fairy story to ignore all of it. "Norah, I tried myself—on more than one occasion—to warn him about those men he'd befriended. He laughed me off, even accused me of jealousy as if I yearned to spend my time losing money at the gambling tables and stumbling home inebriated." He bit off the rest of what was on the tip of his tongue, not wanting to shock her with the sort of life her brother was living in those months preceding his arrest.

But Norah's face registered no such emotion. In fact, she still looked entirely certain of herself—and her brother.

"So the company he kept means he must have attempted to rob that train and . . . and . . . killed that man?" She raised her chin as she held his gaze.

And Stuart couldn't look away from her. She was defiance personified, entirely certain of herself, and he couldn't bear to see that life snuffed out of her once again.

Besides, her reasoning made sense, never mind that there were a hundred other pieces of evidence against Jeremy. "I suppose not," he finally said, and she seemed to glow in response.

She stepped forward, stopping just in front of him. "You'll agree with me that something seemed strange with him today, won't you?"

She blinked at him with those eyes that read more brown than blue in this dimly lit room, and Stuart thought for a moment that he'd agree to anything she suggested, as foolhardy or dangerous as it might be.

*Get a hold of yourself.* He forced himself to look away from her and take a step back—it was the only way he could clear his head. Although when precisely Norah Parker had begun to have that effect on him, he had no idea.

He could feel her eyes on him now, waiting for an answer. The fog lifting from his mind some, he thought back to Jeremy's presence in this room. He'd acted cowed, in a way. He spoke quietly. And he refused to explain himself when offered the chance. Stuart turned to answer Norah's question when the door opened.

"If you'll come with me, miss. Sir." The guard held the door open.

Stuart took up Norah's arm again, tucking her safely against him. But this time felt different. It was as if he were aware of every place her body touched his. He walked stiffly, trying to avoid too much contact. She glanced up at him as they approached the tall stone wall that separated the prison from the town.

"Is there something wrong?" she asked.

Stuart winced inwardly as he shook his head. She'd noticed, and he was being ridiculous. She was Jeremy's little sister, for heaven's sake. Ruthann's closest friend. He'd known her since they were children, when she'd been a pesky tagalong with Ruthann, interrupting all the mischief he, Jeremy, and Nate had tried to find for themselves.

And yet as one of the guards gave her a friendly smile when they passed through the gate, he thought he might like to punch the fellow right in his teeth.

Stuart closed his eyes briefly to clear his head. Out here, past the walls of the prison and on the road back into town, he felt as if he could think better. How Jeremy had an intact thought at all within that place was beyond him. He shuddered to think how many years his former friend would have to withstand behind those walls.

They were approaching the first buildings in town when Norah stopped suddenly and stepped in front of him. "You do agree with me, don't you? That Jeremy was acting strangely?"

"Yes," Stuart confessed.

"He wouldn't share a word about what happened that night, and I don't think it was to spare me. If the details were something he didn't think fit for me to hear, he would have said as much." Her eyes moved past him, back to where he knew she could see the prison over his shoulder.

"I agree." He wished he didn't, but it was obvious Jeremy was keeping something from them, guilty or not. But why?

"I wish I knew why," Norah said softly, echoing Stuart's thoughts. Her gaze found him again, and her expression was determined. "I'm going to find out."

"Norah, I don't think—" Stuart started.

"I want you to help me." She took his hand between her own, heedless of anyone who might be watching. "Please, Stuart."

He dragged his thoughts from how warm her hands were around his and forced himself to look her in the eyes. "Why not Charles? Surely he has an interest in seeing his brother exonerated?"

Norah shook her head. "He's far too busy with his work and distracted by the baby coming. Besides, all I'd get from him is a lecture on how much danger I put myself in and how he won't see it happen again." She paused. "I appreciate that you didn't say a word about danger or tell me the prison isn't a fit place for a lady."

"I figured it was pointless to tell you something you already knew."

She gave him such a winsome smile that he couldn't help but return it.

"But I'd be a poor excuse for a friend if I didn't warn you that there's likely a reason Jeremy wouldn't speak of the details." Whether that was a reason beyond being guilty and not wishing to spin even more lies for his sister, Stuart didn't know. But he kept that thought to himself.

"And that's why I need your help." Her lips pressed together, as if she were forcing herself to hold back tears. "I can't let him remain in that place until we're old and gray. I *can't*. Not without at least making an effort to prove him innocent. You'll help me, won't you, Stuart?"

That look of sorrow in her eyes would be his undoing. Letting her go on wondering would be cruel. It would be far better if she could accept that Jeremy wasn't the brother she'd known and loved. Then she could move on and try to enjoy life again, as he and everyone else was trying to do.

"Yes," he said, hoping he wasn't making a grave mistake. "I'll help you."

"Oh, Stuart! I could hug you! But I won't, or else I'll find myself joining Sissy Flagler as the town's favorite topic of gossip." She gave a laugh and moved back to his side, tucking her arm around his again.

"You could stand on your head in the middle of church and fling piles of horse dung at passersby on the street, and I still don't think you could edge out Miss Flagler as the talk of the town," Stuart said with a laugh. Tongues wagged for months over her involvement with the man who'd tried to destroy Nate's reputation and business last year.

Norah laughed again, and the sound seemed to be just what Stuart needed to hear.

"Thank you," she said, her eyes shining and her face lit in a glow of hope and happiness.

He couldn't say anything for a moment. The words stuck in his throat as he wondered how—and when, exactly—little Norah Parker had grown so beautiful.

"You're welcome," he said as he forced the thought from his head. She was his sister's closest friend, and that was all.

As a friend, he would help her. And then he'd be there to help when she learned the truth about her brother.

# Chapter Five

"TELL ME, STUART, HOW are you keeping up with the increase in business?" Papa rested his fork on his plate as he turned the topic of the dinner conversation from his latest adventures in doctoring sick horses.

"It's been difficult, but we'd rather have more business than we can handle than not enough," Stuart replied.

Charles, who was visiting for dinner with Mary, asked another business-related question, while Mama and Mary discussed plans for making baby clothes. This—thankfully—left Norah alone with her thoughts.

She speared a bite of potato as she thought—yet again—of how oddly Stuart had looked at her as they'd walked home from the prison. He'd eyed her as if he'd never seen her before. It was the strangest thing, and she'd hoped to have some time alone to think it over. Well, that and her plans for uncovering whatever it was that Jeremy was hiding.

But instead, Mama had met them the second Norah stepped inside and insisted Stuart stay for supper. Stuart had heartily accepted the invitation, and for a moment, as they all sat around the table, it had felt like old times.

Only Jeremy was missing.

His absence had been a hole in her heart for so long, and finally—*finally*—she was going to do something about it. She would figure out what had happened, and she would prove his innocence. He'd be released, all would be forgiven, and their lives could all return to normal.

She smiled down at her potatoes and cabbage and beef as she thought of it. And it was all thanks to Stuart.

Norah snuck a glance up at him now. He was laughing at something Charles had said, and one might never know that he'd just squired her over to the Territorial Prison, against every single one of her father's wishes. Stuart had sat here at her family's table so many times, and yet he somehow looked different this time. She tilted her head as she chewed, trying to figure it out.

He was no taller than he'd been two or three or even five years ago. He'd always been clean-shaven, eschewing the current fashion that most men sported. His eyes were no different, nor was his laugh.

Then what was it?

She couldn't nail down a single change, and yet his presence here *felt* different. It was as if *she* were seeing him differently. As if he were a handsome man come to court her rather than her brother's friend.

The thought made Norah drop her fork. It clattered against her plate, causing Mama and Mary to startle.

"Pardon me," she managed to say, but the second they'd resumed their conversation, her eyes found Stuart again.

He was watching her.

Norah's breath caught in her throat. He couldn't *know* what she was thinking, could he?

It was impossible, and yet he gave her a conspiratorial smile before quickly turning his attention back to her father.

Norah sat back, resisting the urge to fan herself. It had grown suddenly warm in the dining room, and her thoughts jumbled together. For the love of all that was good, she needed to get a hold of herself. Stuart was simply being a friend to her. A friend who was far too much of a gentleman to endanger that friendship. Besides, he likely had his pick of ladies. He was much too good-looking, too jovial, and too well-positioned not to.

Yet as she picked her fork up again, her mind wandered back to that smile he'd just given her, the way his hand had felt between hers when she'd taken it up without thinking outside on the street, and every other moment they'd ever spent together. She was reliving the dance he'd asked her for back at the church social the summer before last when she realized Mama was saying her name.

She blinked and found everyone's eyes on her. Her cheeks went warm at the attention, and she barely sputtered out, "Yes, Mama?"

"Mary was asking whether you'd had an enjoyable afternoon visiting with Ruthann?" Mama tilted her head, concern tracing her features. "Are you feeling well enough?"

"Yes, I . . ." Norah laid a hand against her cheek and then dropped it as she straightened in her chair. "I'm perfectly well. And yes, Mary, I did enjoy my visit. Baby Caleb is growing so quickly." She pointedly kept her eyes from Stuart, although she could feel his on her.

Mama gave Stuart a gracious smile. "I'm glad. It was very thoughtful of you to bring Norah home, Stuart."

"We had an enjoyable walk from my sister's," Stuart replied.

"You must feel free to come by any time," Mama said with a look in her eyes that Norah had only seen once before—when Mr. Price had come courting, back before Jeremy had been arrested. It was the same look she'd seen in Stuart's mother's eyes when Mrs. Joliet had decided that Norah needed a young man last summer. Mrs. Joliet must have introduced her to half the young men in town with that matchmaking gleam in her eye.

"It does Norah good to get out and visit. Perhaps she would do more of it if she had a young man to escort her." Mama gave Stuart a broad smile.

Embarrassment curled like hot fire through Norah. She ducked her head as her cheeks flamed, but not before she'd seen the look of terror that had briefly crossed Stuart's face.

Mama *had* to choose Stuart to pin her hopes and dreams for her daughter. Of all the men in town—and there were many!—she picked Ruthann's brother. The boy Norah had known forever.

Norah couldn't possibly have been more mortified.

The conversation continued on as if no one but Norah and Stuart had caught wind of Mama's machinations. After sufficient time had passed—and after Norah thought her cheeks might have returned to a normal shade—she snuck a glance up at Stuart.

He was watching her father as if he were absolutely fascinated by the ins and outs of doctoring horses. And he was pointedly avoiding looking at her.

Norah sat back and released a silent sigh. It was just as well. Her thoughts had been running wild over something she wasn't entirely certain of herself, much less anything that could actually happen. And now Mama had pressed the issue, and Norah had her answer.

Which was all well and good. Her sole focus ought to be Jeremy, anyway. Once she'd succeeded in proving he didn't belong in prison, then she could consider things such as beaux and flirting again.

With someone *other* than Ruthann's brother.

# Chapter Six

THE AFTERNOON SUN STREAMED into the depot, lighting up the dusty corners and illuminating the bits of dirt that passengers had tracked inside. The waiting room was empty now, although a few people still strolled about the platform.

It was the perfect opportunity to speak with the stationmaster—Jeremy's former employer.

The man stood behind the counter, muttering under his breath as he counted something spread out on the counter in front of him. Stuart hesitated. Gerald Rose was awfully busy . . .

*No*. He needed to speak with the man.

Norah had no idea he was here. He couldn't bring himself to speak with her after Mrs. Parker's blatant matchmaking attempt at dinner last night. Just the thought of Norah's turning scarlet from hairline to neckline made him pull at his collar. Even worse, after the initial embarrassment had worn off, all he could think about was how it was impossible to tell what Norah thought of the idea.

And then he'd spent half the night trying to force the thought from his head.

Thankfully, thoughts of Norah and wondering about what she thought of him had diminished as he'd thrown himself into work at Joliet's Cañon City Shipping and Freight. He'd done more work in one morning than he'd accomplished all week. He'd been about to lose himself in tallying the week's receipts when Papa had essentially pushed him out the door, saying he hadn't even gotten all the receipts pulled together, and besides, there was still one more shipment due in on the last train from Santa Fe.

At a loss for how else to spend his time, Stuart had found himself here at the depot. If he'd promised to help Norah, he'd best get on with it. The sooner he showed her evidence of Jeremy's wrongdoing, the sooner she could drop all of this nonsense about his innocence.

He stepped up to the counter. "Pardon me, Mr. Rose?"

The older man looked up from his counting. Stubs of tickets lay spread out before him. A smile spread across his face. "Stuart, it's good to see you. You're here early. That Santa Fe run isn't due in until seven o'clock."

"I'm not here for the shipment. It's . . . well . . ." Why hadn't he taken a moment to compose his thoughts? To think of some less awkward way of inquiring after Mr. Rose's former employee. He glanced around—why, precisely, he didn't know. Except it felt as if any conversation about Jeremy needed to occur in private. He forged ahead. "I've come to ask you about Jeremy Parker."

Mr. Rose's friendly smile instantly disappeared. He shook his head. "Messy business that was. A shame, too. An utter shame."

Stuart clasped his hands behind his back, trying to think of how to ask what he wanted to know. "Jeremy was a friend of mine. I'm not sure if you knew that?"

The man's face crinkled into a sad smile. "It would be hard to forget you boys running across my platform."

The memory sparked a smile for Stuart too. It seemed so long ago, back when neither of them had a care in the world beyond whatever fun they could find that day. "I suppose I'm still thinking about it all. Still trying to piece together where everything went wrong." And wasn't that the truth. Although he'd put the questions to rest long ago, and given up trying to figure it out.

Until Norah.

"I was wondering if you remembered Jeremy acting differently before the robbery attempt. Did he say or do anything that surprised you or that felt out of character for him?"

Mr. Rose pressed his hands against the counter. "I told the judge this, and I'll tell you too. I don't, in fact. Aside from one visit from that no account fellow—Maddox, his name was, the one Jeremy had taken to meeting up with at the Archer House—remember him?"

Stuart tried his best not to scowl. He remembered Tip Maddox all too well. In fact, he'd seen the man from time to time since then, looking as unsavory as ever. Stuart gave Mr. Rose a short nod.

"That Maddox fellow only came by here once, though. I think Jeremy knew I didn't care for the man. Besides that, Jeremy was as he usually was. Punctual, friendly, and a hard worker. I thought he'd take on my duties when I finally decided I'd had enough." Mr. Rose shrugged. "But he spent more and more time with Maddox and those other fellows, and although his work never suffered, I feared he was headed down the wrong road. Sure enough . . ."

He didn't need to say any more. Stuart wholeheartedly agreed with him. He'd found himself without a friend as Jeremy spent more and more of his free time at the saloons and gambling halls with Maddox and the others.

"I told the judge that too." Mr. Rose shook his head. "Hated saying it, but it needed being said. It was awfully clear he'd taken advantage of his work here and a man had to die for it."

Stuart paused. "What do you mean that it was awfully clear?"

"Who else could it have been? Jeremy had spent all his money on cards and drink. More than one man said he owed money. And the sheriff arrived and found Jeremy by the train and that man dead. He was the only one here. There wasn't anyone else it could have been."

Stuart drew in a deep breath and thanked Mr. Rose. It was exactly what he'd heard had happened. Mr. Rose was right—it was indeed awfully clear that Jeremy was the only person who could have planned the half-executed robbery and shot that railroadman.

Stuart stepped outside, wondering why he didn't feel more vindicated that Mr. Rose's story agreed with everything Stuart had thought about the situation.

Instead he felt . . . disappointed.

But what had he expected? For Mr. Rose to toss aside the testimony he'd given in court, and that Stuart had—against his better judgment—read about in the newspaper?

Seeing Jeremy had gotten under his skin. *Norah* had gotten into his head. If he could keep his mind straight, he'd remember that Jeremy had been the one to throw his life away, even before the robbery. And look where it had gotten him.

There was right, and there was wrong, and Jeremy had crossed the line.

Stuart pushed back his shoulders, letting the regrets that sat heavy slide off. They'd be back, although he wished they'd go for good. He hadn't been able to convince Jeremy to stop, and it was no good replaying it all in his head yet again.

He began walking with no specific direction in mind. If he went home, Ma would fuss over him working too hard. He wasn't entirely ready to see Norah yet, particularly if he had to convey to her what Mr. Rose had to say. He was passing a competing shipping and freight business when he spotted Nate, who had his photography equipment set up outside the business.

Stuart's thoughts must have been evident in his expression because Nate immediately straightened up from behind the camera and said, "What happened?"

Stuart relayed what the stationmaster had told him. "It's no different from what I already knew. I don't know why it's got me so unsettled. I suppose it's because I have to tell Norah."

Nate watched him a moment, clearly thinking. "Could be. Or was it the visit you paid to Jeremy yesterday?"

Stuart let out a deep breath and nodded. "It was strange, seeing him again."

Nate adjusted the camera on the tripod. "How was he?"

"Thin. Grateful." Stuart paused, trying to decide how he would describe the way Jeremy avoided speaking about what had happened the night of the robbery. "Norah asked him specifically about what had happened that evening he'd been arrested. He claimed his innocence but refused to say more. And it wasn't as if he didn't want his sister to hear the details—it was something more. I thought maybe it was because he was lying to her, but . . . I don't know. It hasn't sat right with me ever since."

Nate furrowed his brow. "If he says he did nothing wrong, I don't understand why he wouldn't be more forthcoming."

Stuart nodded as Nate leaned down to peer through the camera. "Are you photographing the building?"

Nate straightened again. "Guelph's hired me," he said, nodding at the shipping and freight business that was the largest of the Parkers' many competitors in town. "They want to place an advertisement in the newspaper with an image of their offices."

"Interesting." Stuart considered the idea as Nate adjusted the camera again. It was a novel thought, and one on which he doubted Papa would spend the money. There was plenty of business to go around, but they were always hungry for more, and he had to admire Guelph's for trying something new in their advertising.

"Ever since I came back to town and learned what happened, it's bothered me how abruptly Jeremy changed," Nate said.

"It wasn't abrupt, but yes, it was like a train speeding from the station. I tried to catch up with it, but he was beyond my reach." It still smarted, thinking about how Jeremy had brushed him off, time and again. A man could only take so much of being pushed aside before he walked away for good. And that was exactly what Stuart had to do.

Nate studied the building in front of them, seemingly lost in thought as a couple strolled by on the board sidewalk, hand in hand. Another few people had passed by before Nate spoke again. "I'd like to see him myself. I mentioned it to Ruthann some time ago, but I needed to think it through. Do you suppose he'd be open to seeing me?"

Stuart shrugged. "I can't see why not. He certainly was happy enough to visit with Norah and me." He paused, guilt creeping in through the cracks in his conscience. "I doubt he'd had a single visitor before yesterday."

After a second, Nate nodded. "All right. You ought to come with me. He might have more to say with two old friends than with his sister present."

It was the last thing Stuart wanted to do, but he found himself agreeing with Nate. It would make Norah happy, particularly after he'd told her about his visit with Mr. Rose. And especially if he could scare up some crumb of information from Jeremy to share with her.

After making plans to visit the next day, Stuart left Nate to finish his work. It was time to see Norah again.

He could only hope Mrs. Parker was otherwise occupied—else he might find himself the object of her matchmaking again. He straightened his tie and set out for Norah's house, determined not to let those stray, unasked for thoughts about her enter his mind again.

He was helping a *friend*, and that was all there was to it.

# Chapter Seven

THE MUCK OF THE STREET nearly pulled Norah's shoe right off her foot.

She tugged at the rope that was attached to the cow's . . . harness? Halter? Norah hadn't a clue about the leather contraption around the cow's head. She didn't know the first thing about cows at all, except they made milk and that this one liked to say "moo" more frequently than she thought was probably healthy.

And that this cow—Jilly, according to the note Mr. Beck had sent with her—despised walking.

"Lady, you need to get that animal out of the middle of the road." A surly looking fellow driving a wagon said as he somehow managed to pass by her and the cow.

"I'm trying!" Her voice rose embarrassingly as she tugged on the rope again. The cow didn't move an inch, and the wagon driver merely shook his head and continued on his way.

She looked down at her ruined shoes. Why hadn't she run inside and put on a pair of boots instead? Oh yes, because a cow was standing in the road outside her home. Yet another gift from Mr. Beck. And not a soul had been home to help her. Papa, with his expertise on horses, would have been most helpful, but he'd been gone all day.

And so here she was, in the middle of the road, halfway through town and a block from Mr. Beck's house, with a cow named Jilly who refused to budge.

Swallowing the panic rising in her throat, Norah took a deep breath. Perhaps if she asked the animal nicely rather than tugging at her. After all, *she* wouldn't want to do anything someone ordered her to do. Maybe Jilly was the same way.

"Hello, sweet girl," she said in a calm, soothing voice. Norah raised a hand to scratch Jilly gently on the nose.

Jilly stood completely still, and her big, brown eyes shut just a little.

Norah could have laughed. The cow clearly liked being petted. She kept scratching Jilly's nose as she cooed, "You want to come on down the street with me now, don't you, Miss Jilly? We'll go see your friend, Mr. Beck. I'm sure he has something good for you to eat. Maybe . . . apples. Or oats." Horses liked apples and oats. Whether cows did, Norah didn't know, but it seemed to be working. When she gently pulled on the rope, Jilly took a couple of steps forward.

Sending up a prayer of thanks, Norah continued scratching Jilly's nose and promising everything to the animal from tasty treats to a cozy stall in a barn to a fancy new dress.

And then—*finally*—they reached Mr. Beck's small home.

Norah tied the rope to the handrail on the front steps, although she wasn't certain how necessary that was considering the cow hardly appeared likely to go racing off down the street. She climbed the steps and knocked before going back down to stand near the cow. The last thing she wanted was Mr. Beck inviting her inside for a visit, and so she figured if she looked as if she were in a hurry, that would be less likely to happen.

"Miss Parker!" Mr. Beck, his silver-streaked brown hair glinting in the sun, beamed at her. He shut the door behind him and came down to stand beside her. "You've received my gift. I saw Jilly and thought she was perfect for you." He pushed his spectacles into place and waited for her response.

"Thank you, Mr. Beck. It certainly was a . . . generous gift. But you must know we have no place to keep a cow." She paused and tried to make her voice as gentle as possible. "And please, I've asked you to cease sending me gifts. Don't you remember?"

"Yes, but don't all women do that?" He smiled at her as if she were a ninny who didn't know her own mind.

Norah dug her fingers into her palms. The gifts had been amusing—until the cow—but enough was enough. The first time she'd had to tell Mr. Beck to please not send her any gifts, she'd been terrified of breaking his heart. The second time, she'd felt bad for him. The seventh time held an undercurrent of annoyance. But now?

Now she was mad.

"Mr. Beck, you must stop. I will not accept any more of your gifts."

"My dear Miss Parker," he said fervently, his graying whiskers twitching. "I won't stop until I've won your heart!" He reached for her hand, which she yanked away immediately.

Why wouldn't he *listen* to her? She despised having to be so cruel, but it seemed the only way. "That will never happen."

"Oh, but it will!" He took a step toward her, and she immediately took one backward.

"It will not," a masculine voice said from behind Norah.

Norah swallowed a gasp as Stuart's arm wrapped around her waist. She looked up at him, but he had his eyes on Mr. Beck.

Mr. Beck glanced between them, appearing just as confused as Norah felt. He opened his mouth, but no words came out.

"I must reiterate my intended's request for you to cease sending her gifts. It's unseemly, Beck, don't you agree?" Stuart's voice was as smooth as honey.

Meanwhile, Norah stared at him. His *intended*? Her heart thumped so hard she wondered how the entire street didn't hear it. He must have overheard her conversation with Mr. Beck. The older man would never stop pursuing her . . . but if she were engaged to married to another man . . .

Stuart was a genius. A genius *and* a gallant knight, who'd come to her rescue.

Norah swallowed her surprise, letting a true expression of gratitude and admiration place a smile onto her face.

Mr. Beck inclined his head. "I apologize, Mr. Joliet. I didn't know— I didn't realize . . ." His face turned pink with embarrassment. "Miss Parker, I wish you'd told me."

*I told you to stop sending me gifts!* Norah bit back her frustration and instead gave a dazzling smile to Stuart. "Well, it's so very new and I . . . I simply didn't think about it."

"I wish you both the very best," Mr. Beck said stiffly. His eyes lingered on Norah. She couldn't figure out if he was wistful or suspicious, and she fought the urge to shift her weight from one foot to the other.

"My dear, you're looking very pale. Let me escort you home." Stuart's arm tightened protectively around her waist, as if she needed his support to keep from fainting in the street.

Norah nodded, although she felt perfectly fine. Well, perfectly fine except for the fact that she was now acutely aware of Stuart's arm around her and how that action had pressed her flush against his side.

Perhaps she wasn't feeling so well at all, not with him this close.

"I bid you a good afternoon," Mr. Beck said as Stuart wrapped his free hand around Norah's arm and led her away.

He held her like that until they turned left on the next street, passing a few curious looks as people went to and from their homes. When they turned the corner, Stuart let her go.

"Are you all right?" he asked.

Norah paused beside the home on the corner, feeling strangely out of breath. She'd been so conscious of Stuart's hand pressed against her waist and his side against hers that she felt now like a boat released from anchor. Finally, she nodded.

"Thank you for coming to my rescue," she managed to say. Then she giggled, an impulsive act that seemed to rise from the churn of emotions deep inside. "He gave me cow! A *cow*!"

Stuart laughed too, even as he shook his head. "Ruthann regaled me with his earlier gifts. Perhaps he can find a nice widowed farmer lady to court now."

Feeling much more herself now that Stuart was a couple of steps away, Norah straightened. "Thank you again. I fear we really will now be the topic of gossip—and that's without me standing on my head in the middle of a church service." Between Mr. Beck thinking they were engaged and the looks from more than one curious passerby as Stuart nearly carried her away down the street, gossip was almost certain.

Stuart smirked and held out his arm. When she took it and they began to walk, he said, "Let them talk. It was worthwhile to be freed from the ardent pursuit of Francis Beck, was it not?"

"Oh, certainly! But I worry more about you than myself. Won't that . . . What if word comes back to . . . Well, if you're courting anyone, I'd hate to see her be made upset." It was quite possibly the most awkward thing Norah had ever said. She bit down hard on her lip to keep her cheeks from flaming, and then glanced up at him, far too curious than she ought to be to see his response.

He kept his gaze focused straight ahead, saying, "You needn't worry. No idle chatter will ruin any plans of mine."

Norah looked down to hide the smile that bloomed across her face. How Stuart didn't have any serious prospects was baffling. She'd seen the way other girls had watched him at social events, and he hadn't been shy when it came to conversation or dancing.

And yet here he was, whisking her away from Mr. Beck in an embrace that would send tongues wagging across town—and he didn't seem to mind one bit.

What that meant, she didn't know, and she didn't dare think on it for too long.

Thankfully, Stuart distracted her immediately. "I spoke with the stationmaster earlier today but learned nothing new. Nate and I are going to pay a visit to Jeremy. Nate seems to think he might be more forthcoming with the two of us."

Norah looked up at him, surprised he'd already done so much. "I think that's a wonderful idea. When will you go?"

"Tomorrow. And don't worry, I'll let you know the outcome of the visit as soon as I can." He gave her a smile that warmed her from her toes to her face.

Perhaps tomorrow she would finally know more. All she wanted was for Jeremy to come home again. For her family to be made whole.

And Norah tried desperately to remember that as she fought to keep from losing herself in Stuart's smile.

# Chapter Eight

"YOU WERE HERE JUST the other day." The prison guard's tone was bored, but Stuart knew he wouldn't point out such a fact without it having a purpose.

"Yes, with Mr. Parker's sister. This is another friend of his." Stuart gestured at Nate. "He hasn't visited yet."

The guard eyed them both before resting his gaze back on Stuart. "Visiting's allowed once every three months. He can come in, but not you."

"Yet you'll allow people who want a tour and a way to ease their souls about their own station in life to come in as often as they like." Stuart held the man's gaze. "Provided they pay, of course."

For a moment, Stuart thought the guard wouldn't budge from his position. "All right. You pay again, you can visit. But I don't want to see you back here for another three months."

Stuart fished some coins from his pocket and handed them over. Nate did the same. The guard looked at the money, nodded, and after placing the coins in his pocket, led Stuart and Nate to the same empty, dim room and locked them in.

Nate stared hard at the door once the guard left, clearly uneasy.

"It won't take long," Stuart said.

Nate nodded once, but his fists remained clenched at his sides until the guard returned with Jeremy.

Jeremy appeared much the same as before—healthy enough, but with a hollow sort of look in his eyes. Even when he saw Stuart and Nate, the genuine smile he gave didn't entirely erase the resignation he clearly carried with him.

There were two chairs on the opposite side of the table this time, and—directed by the guard—both Nate and Stuart sat. Stuart waited until the guard took up residence in his corner before speaking.

"I told Nate about the visit Norah and I paid, and he wished to see you also." He kept his eyes on Jeremy as he spoke, searching for some clue that would prove or disprove his tale of innocence.

"It's good to see you both," Jeremy said. "How is my sister?"

"She's well. I believe we finally chased off Francis Beck for good." Stuart sat back in his chair, pleased with himself and yet wondering why he'd mentioned this to Jeremy.

"Beck?" Jeremy gave him a puzzled expression. "Why, he's older than our father."

"Indeed." Stuart closed his mouth before the words he wanted to say fell out. *You should have been there. It was your duty to chase off your sister's unwanted suitors.* Goodness knew how many useless men bent on courting Ruthann he'd turned away before she married Nate. Charles was busy with his own growing family; it should have been Jeremy's responsibility to see Norah had visits from decent men.

Would he have considered Stuart a decent prospect?

Now *that* was a ludicrous thought. And here he was, thinking it. Even as Nate asked Jeremy whether he had enough to eat and decent clothing to wear, Stuart couldn't shake the thought of courting Norah from his head.

His thoughts about Norah had been verging away from friendship into something else lately, but he was hardly courting her—although it would certainly please her mother. And he certainly would never do anything that would put her reputation at risk.

Well, aside from looking very cozy with her on the street yesterday, but that was for a very good reason.

"Stuart paid a visit to the depot yesterday." Nate's words yanked Stuart's attention back into the moment. "He spoke with Mr. Rose."

Jeremy's face remained impassive, but sadness seemed to spark in his eyes, drowning that empty look he'd carried in with him. "How is he?"

"He's well." Stuart leaned forward, laying his arms on the table. "I asked him about you."

Jeremy raised his eyebrows. "Why would you do that?"

"Because your sister is entirely convinced that you're telling her the truth. And she's determined to prove it."

Jeremy stared at him a moment, and then slowly shook his head. "You can't let her do that."

*There it was.*

Stuart glanced at Nate, who looked just as confused as Stuart had felt since his first visit to Jeremy. "And why, pray, can't we?"

Jeremy sat back, silent, his arms crossed.

"I know there's something you aren't sharing with us. Norah does too. And you know her—she's bullheaded enough to follow that belief to the detriment of everything else in her life.

You'd save us all a lot of time if you'd give us a good reason for your claim of innocence." Stuart paused and waited for an answer.

But none was forthcoming.

Stuart pressed his lips together, irritation with Jeremy boiling up from inside. He clenched his hands on the table. "From where I sit, you're guiltier than sin."

"I did nothing wrong that night."

Stuart threw his hands up. "Why should we believe you? The entire town thinks you killed that man."

Jeremy frowned. But still, he remained silent.

"Right. Forget I ever tried to help you." And with that, Stuart stood suddenly, his chair scraping against the floor.

The guard in the corner started forward, looking ready to toss Stuart out the door. Stuart raised his hands, muttered an apology to the guard, and sat again, half-turned away from Jeremy. If the man couldn't tell the truth to his friends, he wasn't someone Stuart wanted to spend time with, much less worry about day after day.

Nate's mouth formed a straight line as he looked away from Stuart and back to Jeremy. He leaned forward, dropping his voice. "It's clear you're keeping something from us. I don't know why, and I don't know what it is. But if it's something that will ease your sister's mind, I suggest you share it with us. Else she'll spend the next twenty-eight years fretting over you and forgetting to live her own life." Nate paused. "And I don't think that's what you want for her."

Jeremy closed his eyes while Stuart looked at Nate with new admiration. He'd known just what to say to get a reaction from Jeremy.

But would it be enough?

"I never meant to hurt anyone." Jeremy opened his eyes. "Least of all my friends and family."

Given how many times Jeremy had dusted him off like an irritating housefly, Stuart was disinclined to believe his old friend had thought of anyone besides himself.

"And that railroadman?" Nate asked quietly.

Jeremy shook his head. "You can't believe me capable of taking a life in that way."

Nate frowned. "A man can do unimaginable things under trying circumstances." Nate's past several years, spent in the Army, had left an indelible and haunted mark on him.

"I didn't pull that trigger." Jeremy held Nate's gaze, unwavering. Determination sat behind the lean lines of his face.

And something inside Stuart gave. Was there the slimmest possibility Jeremy was speaking the truth?

Was Norah right?

"Then who did?" Nate asked.

Jeremy watched him a moment longer, then licked his lips and shook his head. "I can't say."

"Because you don't know or because you don't want to tell us?" Stuart asked.

The question hung in the air.

The silence grew heavy, but Stuart refused to turn away. One glance sideways and he might miss a twitch of the mouth or a dart of a glance that would tell him once and for all whether his old friend could be trusted.

Jeremy leaned forward, dropping his voice to nearly a whisper. "I want to. I wish I could tell the world. But if I did . . ." His eyes shot toward the guard in the corner, whose interest seemed more intent on a speck of dirt on his shirt than on the three other men in the room.

"What?" Stuart finally asked, unable to wait any longer. "For the love of all that's good, Jeremy, tell us why you accepted defeat if you're so innocent?"

"Because they threatened my family!" Jeremy's eyes blazed with a fire so intense it reminded Stuart instantly of Norah.

Stuart blinked at him, the words swirling through his mind as he tried to make sense of them.

"Who?" Nate pressed. "Who made the threats?"

Jeremy shook his head again. "I already said too much."

Nate looked at Stuart, who was still staring at Jeremy. "Is this why you didn't fight? In court, I heard you said you weren't guilty, and yet you did nothing to help yourself."

Shifting in his chair as if it had grown suddenly uncomfortable, Jeremy nodded.

"If you tell us who threatened you, we can help," Nate said.

"I'm not risking my parents' lives, or my sister's, or Charles and Mary's." Jeremy swallowed visibly. "Forget I said anything. I only wanted you to leave here with some amount of respect for me."

Stuart didn't know what he felt—or what he even thought. "What am I supposed to tell Norah?"

"Nothing. Please, don't breathe a word of this to her."

Stuart let out a frustrated breath. Jeremy had no idea how intensely Norah wished to help him. She wouldn't leave it be, no matter what Stuart might say to her. She was after the truth, and not even her parents' rules or Stuart's initial reticence would make her give up.

How in the world was he going to convince her to stop, knowing now what Jeremy had said?

And yet how could he keep the truth from her?

"Stuart. Promise me." Jeremy was watching him, waiting for something Stuart couldn't do.

"I promise I'll keep her safe." That was all he could offer. It was the only thing he could say with certainty.

But it seemed to be enough for Jeremy, because he gave a satisfied nod. "It's best if you don't return here. I don't know who I can trust."

"It was good to see you," Nate said as they stood.

Stuart bade Jeremy goodbye, and they were soon whisked out of the prison and back on the other side of the wall.

"What do you think?" he asked Nate the moment they were clear of the guards.

"He's telling the truth," Nate said without a hint of uncertainty.

Stuart swallowed. Nate was an excellent judge of character. But even without Nate's opinion, Stuart had to admit that it felt as if Jeremy was finally being truthful.

"He's given us absolutely nothing to use to help him," Stuart said as they crossed the street.

Nate lifted his eyebrows.

"You think I'm going to let him turn into a shadow of himself in that place when he didn't commit that murder?"

"Not at all." Nate grinned. "And I take it you aren't keeping a word of this from Norah?"

"Of course not. She deserves to know the truth. All I promised was that I'd keep her safe, and I fully intend to do that."

"Count me in if you need me," Nate said when they arrived at his shop.

Stuart thanked him and began to make his way toward Norah's home. He was just about to bound up the steps to the front door when he paused.

It was nearly supper time. And Mrs. Parker's matchmaking skills would surely be back out in force. He ought to leave and come back tomorrow—sometime when Mrs. Parker was out visiting. Or perhaps he could wait for Norah to leave and happen to join her. Or maybe—

The door opened just then to reveal Mrs. Parker. With a radiant smile, she held out her hand in a gesture of welcome. "Stuart! What a pleasant surprise! Do come in. We're just about to sit down for supper. You may sit right across from Norah."

Stuart groaned inwardly and plastered a smile upon his face. "I'd be delighted to join you, Mrs. Parker. Thank you."

And in he stepped for an evening of awkwardly avoiding looking at Norah—and even more futile attempts at trying not to think about her in ways that would find him in a world of trouble.

# Chapter Nine

"DO STOP FIDGETING," Mama whispered in Norah's ear. "He'll think you're unable to sit through a meal."

"I've known him since I was a child. I'm certain he knows whether or not I can remain still while seated by now," Norah hissed back. She clamped her lips shut when Mama gave her a glare that could have melted candle wax.

She hadn't meant to be so rude. But Mama's obvious attempts at extolling Norah's every virtue were bordering on the ridiculous. In fact, she'd caught Papa nearly choking on a bite of ham when Mama claimed Norah could create the sweetest melodies on the piano. Even Stuart had shown a difficult time keeping a straight face at that nonsense. Norah's hands were clumsy on the keys at best, and Stuart had sat through more than one social occasion when Norah had been persuaded to show off her "talent."

Of course, those occasions were merry anyway, and not the slightest bit awkward. They'd all had a good laugh at Norah's lack of musical talent afterward, far out of the earshot of any mothers. In fact, Norah distinctly remembered Stuart saying that her piano playing reminded him of the annoying buzz of an insect in his ear.

That all felt like so long ago now. Everything that had happened before Jeremy's arrest felt like another life, a brightly lit, amusing life. And now . . .

Norah pressed her lips together and forced herself not to squirm in her chair. At least Papa had rescued the conversation and turned it toward dull matters of business.

"Another freight company opened just the other day, I heard," Papa was saying.

"Indeed. We're lucky there is plenty of business to go around," Stuart replied.

Norah could practically hear her mother's mind spinning as she tried to find a way to turn the talk back toward Norah and all her many talents and virtues.

"I'd wondered just that. You don't fear losing business to any of these other companies? I imagine the competition is strong," Papa said, sitting back comfortably in his chair.

Norah watched her father with envy, wishing she could lean back like that. Why was it that men got all the comforts in life?

"It's certainly competitive, but my father isn't worried, and I suppose that means I'm not either." Stuart replaced his napkin on the table and glanced at Norah.

She fought the urge to squirm again. Not because of his gaze, she told herself, but because she hadn't had an opportunity yet to learn what he might have discovered during his visit to the prison today.

"If it's agreeable to you, Mrs. Parker, I'd like to take Norah out for a short stroll." Stuart gave Mama a smile that no mother in her right mind would ever say no to.

Not that it took much at all for Mama to clap her hands together and agree enthusiastically. "That sounds quite lovely. It's a beautiful evening. It feels as if autumn has arrived. Norah, take a wrap, or else you might be chilled."

Norah would have taken six winter coats, a pair of heavy boots, and a fur muff if it meant she could leave this table and finally speak to Stuart alone.

Guarded against any potential autumn chill and with Stuart's arm securely wrapped around hers, Norah could barely wait until they were away from the house before bursting out with, "And? Did you learn anything new? How was Jeremy? Did he say something useful?"

Stuart smiled at her, his blue eyes lit up in amusement at her barrage of questions. "He's well. He was glad to see Nate." He paused, his expression turning more serious. "We discovered why he refused to say more on the topic of his innocence."

Norah stopped. "Please tell me. What did he say?"

Stuart glanced around them, as if searching for listening ears. The growing shadows of night had begun to blot out the last remaining light of dusk and the windows of the homes nearby flickered with lamps. "He reiterated that he'd done nothing wrong, but that certain men had threatened his family should he fight the charges laid out against him. He also asked me not to tell you." Stuart gave her a wry grin.

Norah's heart beat faster, both at the news and at the way Stuart was looking at her. Her hand tightened instinctively around his arm as she pondered what Jeremy's words meant. "Did he say who had made these threats?" Her voice was barely a whisper.

"He didn't. But we can be sure it's the true guilty party. And I have a strong feeling I know who those men might be." He frowned at that.

Norah swallowed past the lump of fear that had risen in her throat. As glad as she was to have more information about Jeremy, she hadn't expected something so . . . unsettling. "Who? Are they still in town?"

"Jeremy's old 'friends.'" He spoke the last word with a curl of distaste. "I've seen one or two from time to time. They're laying low, but they're around."

Norah's stomach turned. She'd tried hard not to think about those months before Jeremy had been put in jail and tried for murder and robbery. But now they all came rushing back. He'd changed then. Her sweet, funny, carefree brother had been pensive and withdrawn, never home, and when she did see him, he smelled of cigars and whiskey. And those men he must have been spending time with then . . .

They were the ones responsible—for everything.

She pressed a hand against her stomach, trying to hold in the fear and awful memories.

"Norah? Are you all right? I didn't mean to upset you."

Her eyes found Stuart's as his hand gently pried hers away from her stomach and wrapped it safely between his fingers. He extracted his arm from where it had still been wrapped around hers and took her other hand.

She squeezed her eyes shut and let the gentle pressure of Stuart's fingers against her own soothe away the fears of the past.

"It's all right. They don't know he said anything to Nate and me," he said, his voice low and strong. The sound of it eased the worry in her mind, and Norah opened her eyes to find him watching her, his jaw tight with concern.

She opened her mouth to say something, but no sound emerged. Instead, she nodded.

"I promised Jeremy I would keep you safe, and I intend to do that." His eyes held hers with such an intense seriousness that all thought in her head seemed to vanish. She couldn't look away—not that she wanted to. Her body felt pinned to this spot, unable to do anything but accept that look Stuart was giving her.

One thought flickered in her mind, sparking, fading away, and then coming back to life again and forcing its way out into the open. "I won't sit idly by while you do all the work to help Jeremy."

Stuart laughed. "I wouldn't dream of it. But if a situation becomes too dangerous, I hope you'll let me live up to the word I gave your brother."

Norah twisted the corner of her mouth into a mock look of resignation. "If I must."

Stuart shook his head as he let her hands go and took up her arm again. "You're a force to be reckoned with, Norah Parker, and somehow I think Jeremy has forgotten that."

Norah tried to concentrate on Stuart's words instead of how cold her hands felt under her gloves without his wrapped around them. "Jeremy forgot quite a bit in that time before his arrest."

Stuart's face darkened as he led them down the road. "That he did."

They were quiet a moment, and Norah thought on that time. It was odd, the way Jeremy had changed so suddenly. Her father said it was a last attempt at hanging onto boyhood, but Norah hadn't been so certain.

"Don't you think it was strange, the way Jeremy acted all those months before the robbery? How quickly he changed?" she asked.

"It was. I never could determine what was so intriguing about those men he befriended, unless he enjoyed losing all his money and staggering about—" He cut off his words mid-sentence. "I apologize. Norah, I never should have—"

He looked so embarrassed, she had to laugh. "Stuart, are you apologizing for offending my delicate sensibilities?"

"I, well . . . Yes, I suppose I am." He straightened his shoulders even as his face went ruddy.

They turned the corner, entering a part of town with more businesses and shops. Norah nodded to a couple she recognized from church as they passed.

"You needn't worry about that," she said. "I know Jeremy was indulging in some unsavory habits."

When Stuart didn't answer, she looked up at him. His gaze was fixed on something across the road.

"What is it?" she finally asked, curious as to what had him so riveted.

"That's one of the men Jeremy was spending so much time with before . . ." Stuart trailed off, seemingly lost in thought.

Norah squinted through the darkness. A man leaned against the wall of one of the many saloons in town, the lamplight from inside sending a glow over his features. Norah never would have recognized him, but of course, she'd never met any of Jeremy's supposed newer friends. Looking at this man now, she was torn between curiosity and a healthy dose of wariness.

"Do you trust me?"

Norah tore her gaze from the man across the road to meet Stuart's eyes. "Yes," she said without hesitation.

And then, without a word, Stuart began to lead her across the road—directly toward the man in front of the saloon.

# Chapter Ten

"HAWKINS!" STUART BELLOWED out the made-up name as he and Norah were halfway across the street. There was no reaction from the man in front of the saloon, Tip Maddox. Stuart remembered him all too well. He was the dark-haired one. The one who seemed to be ringleader of the whole group of them.

"Hawkins!" Stuart called again when they reached the edge of the street. He paused to let Norah wipe the bottoms of her shoes on the edge of the board sidewalk. "Where have you been?"

Maddox finally looked up. He glanced at Stuart and then looked around, presumably for the imaginary Hawkins. Finding no one, he turned his gaze back to Stuart, his brows furrowed.

"I've been looking for you all day." Norah's arm safely nestled around his own, he stepped forward until he was in front of Maddox. "I wanted to—" He paused suddenly and tilted his head as if he were confused. "I apologize. I thought you were someone else. You haven't seen Reginald Hawkins inside this establishment, by chance?"

"Afraid I don't know the fellow." His eyes traced Stuart in an uninterested manner and quickly hopped to Norah. He briefly touched the brim of his hat in greeting. "I do know this lady, however. Good evening, Miss Parker."

Norah's fingers tightened around his arm, the only sign she gave that Maddox made her nervous. Stuart fought to control his own expression. He knew without a doubt that Maddox was the one who'd made threats against Jeremy's family, and the fact that he recognized Norah was enough to make Stuart wish he'd never had the bright idea to drag her over here in order to attempt to work his way in Maddox's good graces.

"Good evening, sir," Norah said with a gracious smile Stuart knew reached no further than her lips. "I'm afraid you have me at a disadvantage, as I don't believe we've been introduced."

"Tip Maddox. I'm a friend of your brother's." Maddox gave an obnoxious little bow, that cigar still in hand.

"How interesting. I thought I'd met all of Charles's friends."

Stuart bit the inside of his cheek to keep from laughing. Norah was certainly playing up her role.

"Not Charles, but Jeremy. Before . . . well, it's a shame what happened. I'm sorry for any grief he may have caused you." Maddox looked appropriately remorseful.

The man was likely behind everything that had happened to Jeremy, and here he was, playing the innocent to Norah. Stuart had half a mind to let Maddox know exactly what he thought of him, but settled for grinding his teeth together instead. He couldn't ingratiate himself with the man—and learn the truth about how Jeremy found himself in prison—if he called Maddox out right here on the street.

"Thank you," Norah said softly, and Stuart knew it was taking all of her self-control not to show her true emotions. "It's been difficult for my family, but I try to entertain myself with other distractions."

Eager to take the attention off Norah, and to accomplish the task he'd come here for, Stuart nodded at the saloon behind Maddox. "After I take Miss Parker home, I thought I'd stop in for a drink. Perhaps you'd like to join me—and Hawkins," he added lamely, remembering his farce. "A friend of Jeremy's is a friend of mine."

"You must forgive me, but I don't do much in the way of imbibing these days," Maddox said, his gaze returning to Norah. "I find it tends to upset the ladies."

A muscle in Stuart's eyelid twitched. Maddox was far too interested in Norah. He laid his free hand protectively on her arm.

"Of course, and yet most are tolerant of a fellow indulging on occasion," Stuart said.

Norah's eyes shot toward him, and Stuart could have kicked himself. What if she thought him some sort of drunkard now? What had possessed him to say such a thing? Maddox's eyes gleamed as he watched their interaction.

"On the contrary," Norah said, her voice as light as a feather and her eyes focused on Maddox. "I find the scent of whiskey quite repulsive."

Stuart cringed inside, not so much at her words but at the way she was looking at Maddox. She blinked at him, slowly but pointedly, and her smile never faltered. It was as if— As if—

"Miss Parker, I wholeheartedly agree. I would never think of bringing a lady such as yourself near a saloon." Maddox's gaze slid quickly to Stuart to ensure the jab had hit as he'd intended.

"I much prefer to enjoy the theater or a quiet evening conversing in a parlor."

"Oh, I do so enjoy the theater!" Norah was practically gushing.

And Stuart could barely keep his jaw from hanging open. It took everything he had to maintain hold of his dignity and not go dragging Norah off across the road and away from Maddox.

"Perhaps you'd like to accompany me some time?" Maddox didn't waver in his gaze toward Norah at all now. It was as if Stuart wasn't even there.

"I would enjoy that, Mr. Maddox," Norah said demurely.

Stuart mustered up his ability to speak. "If you'll forgive us, I must be getting Miss Parker home." He barely gave Maddox a moment to say goodbye before aiming Norah back across the road.

Once they were safely across the street, Stuart didn't know what question to ask first. In the span of only a few minutes, he'd gone from worrying that he'd put Norah in danger to admiring her ability to playact to questioning whether she was truly interested in a snake like Maddox. "You know who that was, don't you?" he finally managed to say.

"Yes, of course I do. You told me, remember?" Norah's mouth crooked up as if she were amused at Stuart's question.

Stuart waited until they'd turned the corner to stop. "What possessed you to agree to go to the theater with that man?"

She raised her eyebrows. "I thought your goal in pretending to mistake him for someone else was to find a way to ingratiate yourself to him, thereby creating the opportunity to discover the truth of what happened the night of the robbery."

"Yes," he said slowly. "But—"

"Well, he didn't seem to care much for you, but he was certainly showing an interest in me. I wasn't about to let that go to waste." She spoke as if she hadn't just invited the man who'd threatened her entire family to come join her in their parlor for tea and conversation.

"Yes, but . . . it's too dangerous." *And I don't want that man anywhere near you*. All he could hope was that the raging jealousy that was snaking its way through him didn't show.

"I'm aware. Although I suspect all he wants is to learn whether Jeremy has said anything to me. Once I tell him I haven't spoken to my brother, I imagine he'll disappear."

*Unless he's after something else*. Stuart clamped his mouth shut. His jaw ached from the unspoken words. "I don't like it," he finally said as they drew closer to the Parkers' home.

Norah paused at the bottom of the steps that led up to the front door. She looked up at him with shining eyes and a serious expression. "You don't have to. But I'll ensure we're in a public place. Nothing will happen, save for me discerning whether Mr. Maddox and his associates somehow convinced Jeremy to go along with them in breaking the law and set it up so that he was the only one who paid for it."

She was changing the subject, trying to turn his mind back to Jeremy by posing that theory. Stuart sighed. The ball of fear and jealousy that sat lodged in his stomach wouldn't go anywhere until this was over, but it would do no good to try to persuade Norah to give up this scheme.

He'd have to trust her, plain and simple.

"Jeremy wouldn't be as innocent as he claims if he agreed to go along with robbing a train," Stuart said, surrendering to Norah's gentle nudge into a new line of conversation.

"Yes, that's true." Her face scrunched up as she thought, and Stuart thought he'd never seen anything more adorable. Before he realized what he was doing, he'd reached out and run his fingers over her cheek and down to her jaw.

Her face instantly smoothed out as she stiffened. Stuart yanked his hand away. His face burned. What had he done?

And worse, why did she stare at him as if he'd burned her with his touch?

"I'm sorry," he said, his voice strangled as his heart plummeted with the gravest sort of disappointment. "I shouldn't have done that."

Slowly, her lips turned upward. Then, before he could react at all, she'd stepped forward, rose up on the tips of her toes, and planted a kiss on his cheek.

"Good night, Stuart. Thank you for the stroll." And then she was gone, leaving him alone at the bottom of the steps.

His hand instinctively went to his cheek, feeling for the spot on his skin that her lips had touched.

Norah Parker had kissed him.

# Chapter Eleven

BARELY A DAY HAD PASSED before Mr. Tip Maddox came calling.

He arrived early in the evening, asking to escort her to supper at a nearby restaurant. Every instinct inside of Norah recoiled at the very idea, and yet she forced herself to remember Jeremy, to smile, and agree pleasantly.

Mr. Maddox, with his greased dark hair and nearly black eyes, exuded a presence of trouble barely concealed with civility. It hadn't been as noticeable in the dark outside the saloon the night before, but it chilled Norah to her core as he stood in the entryway of her home. Even Mama could feel that something wasn't entirely right with Mr. Maddox. It was evident in the tight smile she gave him and the very reticent way she agreed to allow him to take Norah to supper.

"Please be home immediately afterward," she said from the doorway as they made their way down the stairs. "Else your father will be concerned."

It was both an admonition to Mr. Maddox and a slightly veiled threat if he didn't comply, and Norah was immensely proud of her mother's sly ability to ensure her safety. She was more than certain she'd hear Mama's every thought about Mr. Maddox's unsuitability the moment she arrived home.

And Norah would agree with her completely.

Simply allowing Mr. Maddox to take her arm made her stomach lurch. But she forced yet another smile to her face as he did so and said soothing, ingratiating words to make him think she had an immense interest in him.

It was the only way to help Jeremy, and as long as she kept that in mind, she could withstand this evening with Mr. Maddox.

He was prattling on about business matters without precisely letting on what sort of business he was in. Eventually, curiosity grew the better of Norah, and she asked him as soon as they were settled into seats near the window at the restaurant.

"Oh, I've an interest in several businesses," he said noncommittally. "But I've a particular interest in moving into shipping and freight, as that seems to be a successful sort of business here in Cañon City."

"It is indeed. Many men have done well in that line of work."

The waitress approached at that moment, and as she told them of the dishes available that evening, Norah wondered why Mr. Maddox hadn't been more interested in speaking with Stuart too, given that he worked in an integral position at his family's freight business. Then again, Stuart hadn't introduced himself. Because he'd been far too busy seething over the attention Norah had paid to Mr. Maddox.

She had to look down to keep Mr. Maddox from seeing her flaming cheeks as she remembered Stuart's barely contained jealousy. Every attention she'd shown Mr. Maddox had been pretend, of course, but in no way had she ever expected Stuart's reaction.

It had buoyed her hopes so much that she'd gathered the courage to give him that kiss on the cheek at the end of the evening. And then she'd promptly regretted her impulsiveness and run inside before she could see his reaction. She'd spent half the day hoping he would visit that evening, but of course, if he did now, she would never know.

Because here she was with Mr. Maddox instead.

He must have ordered for her because the waitress was leaving the table. Norah was just realizing that he hadn't bothered to ask her if she cared for the dish he'd chosen, but she couldn't think long on that because he was going on again about the shipping and freight business.

"—so many companies in town," he was saying. "I presume your brother Charles is happy with his position?"

"He is, so far as I know," she said. What an odd question. Was he hoping to find work? If he was involved in the attempted robbery Jeremy went to prison for, Mr. Maddox hardly seemed the sort to take up mundane work at a freight office.

"He's with Guelph's Freight Company, right?" Mr. Maddox asked.

"Yes."

"What sort of work does he do?" He must have realized it was a strange question to ask Charles's sister, because he then added, "I'm considering asking for work there, and it's best to know more about the business before approaching them, you see."

She nodded. It was perfectly reasonable—if she believed he really wanted a job at Charles's company. "He handles the accounts for a few of the silver mines, but that's all I know." She gave a light laugh, as if she had no interest in such matters. "Any more than that, and you'll have to talk to Charles yourself."

"Could you introduce me?" He watched her with curious eyes. "I would like to learn more about the company, and if it goes well, perhaps he could put in a good word for me."

"I . . . I suppose." It was quite possibly the strangest request Norah had ever received from a suitor.

But then again, Mr. Maddox wasn't exactly a suitor. Thankfully.

Their dinner arrived, and Norah was relieved to see it was a simple plate of venison, potatoes, and squash. Mr. Maddox cut into his meat, and before he could carry on about Charles and the freight business, she asked the question that had been most on her mind.

"Mr. Maddox, you said you were a friend of Jeremy's. Tell me, do you believe he is truly guilty of the crimes for which he's been punished?" It was a bold question, one that sat just on the edge of giving away what she knew.

But she wanted to see his reaction.

He carefully finished cutting his venison, and then looked up at her. His face was drawn into a grave expression, one that said he felt nothing but sorrow for her and for Jeremy—but his eyes indicated something else entirely.

She studied them as he spoke, trying to determine the truth that sat in their inky depths.

"His actions surprised me, as I'm sure they did everyone. And yet the evidence against him was strong." Mr. Maddox spoke in a measured tone, his gaze on her the entire time.

He hadn't answered her question. Heart pounding, Norah tightened her grip on her fork, hoping she didn't convey how nervous she was. Every reasonable voice in her head screamed at her to drop the subject, but she forced them back.

There was only one reason she agreed to this outing with the odious Mr. Maddox, and that was to help Jeremy.

And so she pressed on. "You were friendly with him. Did you see him much in the days beforehand?" She tried to keep her voice light, as if she was simply making conversation and trying to get to know Mr. Maddox better.

He gave her a smile that didn't reach his eyes. "I did. I wish I'd known what he was planning. I would have attempted to dissuade him from it."

Norah shoved a bite of potatoes into her mouth to give herself a moment to think before speaking again. As she chewed, an idea emerged. It was a dangerous thought . . . and yet, if it worked, it would make sitting across from Mr. Maddox worthwhile.

"To be honest, Mr. Maddox, I've forgotten a lot about that moment in time. I'm sure it was the shock, and perhaps it's for the best." It was a bald lie. Norah would never forget each terrible second of those moments when she'd learned of Jeremy's arrest—and every awful event afterward. She set her fork down and laced her hands together in her lap, praying for strength and asking forgiveness for the falsehoods she was telling.

"But there is one detail I remember so clearly. The day before the robbery, I had set aside a few bits of jewelry I no longer cared for. It was nothing very dear, of course, but I thought I might see if a few friends would like to have the pieces. Jeremy picked up a necklace—a simple one, but very pretty with a small cameo. He asked if he might give it to a friend who was saving money to buy a gift for the girl he was courting. I agreed, of course. He mentioned the friend's name at the time, but it meant nothing to me then. It was Tip." She gave him her prettiest smile, and then let it falter, as if she was troubled. "I do hope he was able to give it to you before . . ."

Mr. Maddox paused only half a second before giving her a sad smile. "My dear Miss Parker, that gesture was very much like the Jeremy I knew. You'll be pleased to know that he did indeed give me the necklace, and I gave it as a gift that very evening." He paused. "You mustn't trouble yourself over that, though. That courtship is now long in the past."

Norah's heart nearly stopped. She had to force herself to nod and say, "Of course."

She could hardly wait to tell Stuart. Mr. Maddox had just lied to her. And if he was willing to agree to a false story about a necklace, what else was he hiding?

# Chapter Twelve

HE OUGHTN'T HAVE PUT it past Maddox to waste any time in visiting Norah.

When Stuart had stopped by the Parkers' home that evening, dear Mrs. Parker had apologized for Norah's absence. When she'd pressed him for questions about Maddox, who she clearly didn't much care for, he'd done his best to soothe her worries. There was no point in letting her know of the man's true character. Or that he didn't trust Maddox's intentions at all.

Mrs. Parker had thanked him and invited him for supper the following evening. Stuart left feeling awfully good about himself. Mrs. Parker clearly hoped he and Norah might find . . .

What, precisely?

The thought stopped Stuart in his tracks. Love? Marriage? His head spun. He'd barely had time to contemplate anything beyond the constant presence of Norah in his thoughts and the way every hair on his body seemed to stand on end when he'd touched her cheek.

But he did know one thing for certain, and that was the very thought of Maddox taking Norah's arm or whispering in her ear made him want to hit something so badly that he could hardly see straight.

He couldn't go home. Papa would want to talk business, and Ma would ask after Norah—he was beginning to suspect that she'd had more than one conversation with Mrs. Parker about how much time he and Norah were spending together.

He could pay a visit to Nate and Ruthann, but he didn't feel like sitting. Moving helped drive the thoughts of Norah and Maddox from his mind, and besides, he felt he ought to do something to further discover more about what happened the night of the robbery.

Particularly since Norah was doing just that as she pretended to flirt with Maddox.

Stuart curled his hands into fists as he strode down the sidewalk. The sun had set, and with that, the saloons and gambling halls had come alive. He paused outside the one where they'd found Maddox last evening as a thought occurred to him.

If Maddox had been here, his group of associates had probably been inside. And it was possible they were here again tonight.

He pushed open the doors. Inside, the room was hazy with cigar smoke and loud with conversation and the sound of an out-of-tune piano somewhere in the rear. Stuart moved toward the bar as he searched for Maddox's friends. Finally, at the far end of the bar, he spotted a shock of red hair. Only one man he knew had that hair. Sid Chase, Maddox's closest confidant.

As he grew closer to Chase, he began to recognize the other men around him. It was the same group Jeremy had fallen in with in those months before the robbery.

The group for which he'd cast aside his real friends.

Stuart forced himself to swallow those bitter feelings and slid in behind a tall blond fellow whose name he couldn't recall. He ordered a drink from the bartender and pretended to be riveted by the large, dirty mirror that hung behind the bar as he listened to the conversation beside him.

They were speaking of Guelph's Freight Company. One of the men was bragging about being hired on. Stuart truly wondered if old Mr. Guelph had finally lost his mind, giving work to one of these poor excuses for men, but it was a good way to work himself into the conversation.

Particularly when one of the other men noted in a rough sounding voice that he wished he'd been able to get work at Guelph's too.

"If you're wanting to work in the freight business, you ought to try Joliet's. We're in need of a new clerk." He didn't look at them as he spoke, but they heard him all the same.

They were quiet as they turned to look at him. Finally, the man wishing he'd gotten work at Guelph's spoke up.

"You work for Joliet's?" he asked.

Satisfied to finally be funneling the fifty different emotions he felt about Norah into something useful, he turned to face the man who'd spoken. The fellow was short and squat, with some angry looking blemishes on his face. He was hardly the sort you'd want greeting potential customers, with that gruff voice and that wary look in his eye.

"I do. Stuart Joliet." He gave the man a quick nod in lieu of holding out a hand. "You ought to inquire about it at our offices in the morning."

The man looked to the fellow standing next to him before turning back to Stuart with an amused half-smile. "Thank you,

Joliet. I'll do just that." He paused. "Chase over there just start-ed work at Guelph's. You know Guelph's?"

Asking if he knew Guelph's was like asking if he knew his own two hands. But Stuart gave a friendly nod. "I do. Good company."

"They keep accounts with the silver mines. And the coal-fields." Chase added the latter as almost an afterthought. "I haven't heard of Joliet's having customers like that."

*Because we don't feel the need to tell the town about our clients' business.* Guelph's did good work, but they were hardly discreet.

"We keep some larger accounts," Stuart hedged.

"No mines?" the man with the blemishes who was so inter-ested in a job asked.

"Maybe," Stuart said carefully. They were awfully interested in the mines. He tucked that thought away to consider more later. "We pride ourselves on not publicly discussing our clients' businesses."

The squat man frowned, clearly disappointed, while Chase raised his eyebrows.

"One needs to work there to earn this privileged informa-tion," Chase said. "I respect that."

Stuart had the very strong feeling he'd find the short man with rough-sounding voice in their offices tomorrow, asking af-ter a position with the company.

He was about to ask Chase more about his work with Guelph's when Maddox's voice sounded from behind him. He turned around to find the man wearing a fine suit and ordering a whiskey. He'd unknotted the string tie at his throat and had slung his coat over his shoulder.

Maddox's eyes slid immediately to Stuart. "I remember you." He held up his drink as if in a toast. "I must thank you for introducing me to Miss Parker. The lady and I spent an enjoyable evening together."

Stuart dug his nails into his palms as he watched Maddox drink. So much for the man's claim that he didn't indulge in whiskey—not that Stuart had expected him to be a truthful sort. "I didn't introduce you."

Maddox raised his eyebrows in amusement as he set the glass down. "Ah, yes. I remember now. Well, I hate to be the one to disappoint you, but I expect you won't be seeing much of Miss Parker any more."

Maddox was goading him. Stuart knew that, and yet he couldn't keep himself from responding. "And why is that?"

"Surely you can figure that out, Mr. . . .?"

"Joliet," Stuart said.

A spark of curiosity lit in Maddox's eyes, and then quickly fizzled out. That was certainly interesting, and Stuart wondered if it had anything to do with the other men's interest in finding work with shipping and freight companies.

"Miss Parker made it abundantly clear tonight that she much prefers my company to anyone else's. And that includes yours, Joliet." Maddox slid his empty glass across the bar, nodding at the barkeep as he did so. "If you wish to preserve your dignity, you'd best step aside now."

Stuart stared at him, disbelief warring with utter amusement at Maddox's presumption of victory. It flitted through his mind that he wasn't exactly *courting* Norah, but that thought disappeared as soon as it arose. Instead, he took a step forward and looked Maddox right in his dark eyes.

"I'm not a man who gives up easily. And if Norah indicated she preferred you in any way, I imagine you misunderstood her words." He kept his voice even as the rest of his body tightened with barely controlled irritation.

Maddox made no move to straighten at all. Instead, he took the drink the barkeep had set down and gave Stuart a wry smile. "If you knew the liberties *Norah* allowed me, you'd take back everything you just said, tuck your tail, and—"

Stuart didn't allow him to finish. His fist was cutting through the short distance between them before he realized he'd even moved. But it never connected with its target.

A strong hand had wrapped itself around Stuart's arm, holding him back.

Maddox laughed as Stuart jerked his head to the right to find the barkeep reaching over the bar to keep him from smashing his fist into Maddox's face. In the barkeep's free hand was a shotgun, which he raised as he dropped Stuart's arm.

"Get on out. Last thing I need is a fight in here. Fighting brings in the law, and I'll have none of that. You two want to fight, go outside." He motioned the shotgun toward the door.

Maddox held up his hands. "I've got no cause to fight Mr. Joliet. If it's just as well, I'd rather stay here and drink."

The barkeep nodded and swung the shotgun toward Stuart.

"I'm going," Stuart muttered. He didn't give Maddox a second glance as he strode toward the door.

He gulped the fresh air when he stepped outside, letting it clear his mind.

There was only one place he wanted to be right now—one person he wanted to see.

Norah.

# Chapter Thirteen

THE KNOCK AT THE DOOR came just as Norah had bid goodnight to her parents.

She paused in the hallway, the surprise sound making her heart thump faster. Who could be at the door this late?

She glanced down the hall, waiting for Papa to emerge. Under no circumstances would he want her answering the door at this hour.

But he didn't come, and neither did Mama. They must not have heard it.

Norah approached the door, tentatively laying her fingers on the knob. The knock came again, and praying she wasn't making a terrible mistake, she opened it just far enough to peer through the crack into the night.

Stuart stood on the other side, his dark blond hair tousled even more than normal. The light from the lamp Norah held caught his eyes, revealing a slightly wild look.

"Stuart," Norah whispered, and glancing down the empty hallway, she stepped outside so as not to alarm her parents. "It's late. Why are you here?"

"I had to see you." His voice was frayed at the edges. He looked her over, and seemingly satisfied, he shoved his hands into his trousers pockets. "I'm sorry. I shouldn't have come. I didn't realize the time."

Norah set the lamp down. "Did something happen?"

He gave a sharp laugh. "I'd planned to ask you the same."

"What do you mean? All is well here. Aside from the perfectly awful supper I endured with Mr. Maddox, that is." She shuddered at the thought of him.

Stuart studied her a moment. "He didn't . . . He wasn't impolite?"

"Not particularly. But I hope never to have to spend another moment in his presence. There's simply something . . . wrong about him."

Stuart looked relieved, letting out a breath and turning his head to look down the street.

Warmth bloomed inside Norah's heart. He'd worried over her. She bit back a smile. "I am glad you came. I was bursting with the desire to tell you what I learned."

His eyes found her again, and he looked much more relaxed than he had when he arrived. He took his hands from his pockets and leaned one on the iron railing. "Mr. Maddox shared something of interest?"

She nodded. "Indeed. First, I proved him to be a liar. After he told me how full of sorrow he was that he couldn't stop Jeremy from trying to rob that train, I spun a tale about a necklace Jeremy had requested from me to give to Mr. Maddox for his sweetheart. I told him I hoped he received it, and he told me he had. I could hardly believe it! He must be hiding more about that night."

Stuart watched her with an expression of proud disbelief. "Did he reveal anything else?"

"Nothing of particular usefulness. He spent most of the conversation asking me about Charles and his work at Guelph's."

Stuart stood up straight. "That's interesting. I just came from that saloon we found Maddox in front of last night. I thought I could talk with his associates, see what they might have to say." He added that part quickly, as if he felt he needed to explain his presence in a saloon. "They were also very interested in Guelph's, as one fellow had just started work there. I mentioned they might also find work at Joliet's, and they were more curious about the accounts we held than in the requirements of the position."

Norah scrunched up her forehead as a chilly breeze sent her skirts rustling. "You don't suppose . . ." She trailed off, not entirely certain if she was piecing together facts that didn't exist.

"That they're planning something involving Guelph's," Stuart finished for her. "And the mines. They were very interested in the mines. And knowing those men, it's not something good."

Norah chewed her lip. "You don't suppose this all has something to do with Jeremy and the robbery?"

"The thought crossed my mind, although I don't know how or why. Perhaps they're simply planning another robbery."

A terrible thought occurred to Norah. No, she couldn't do that again. Just the idea of it made her feel ill. But . . . it might give them the answers they needed. "I'll spend more time with Mr. Maddox," she forced herself to say.

Stuart's face turned to stone. "No. Absolutely not. I . . . I would never ask you to do that."

"You don't need to," Norah replied, slightly chagrined. "I thought of the idea myself, and I'm quite capable of making my own decisions."

He shook his head. "It's too dangerous."

"It's the only way we can discover more. He likes me. I can get him to tell me something useful." She could, if her face didn't betray precisely how she felt about it.

"Norah." Stuart's hand clamped around her wrist. "I can't—I won't let you endanger yourself. I—" He paused and swallowed. "Jeremy would never forgive me if I allowed it."

*Jeremy* wouldn't forgive him? Norah's annoyance slipped away as she realized this had nothing to do with Jeremy or the danger involved.

"Stuart," she said softly, her cheeks growing warm with what she was about to say.

"Yes?"

She slid her wrist from his grasp, but stopped when her hand met his. He intertwined his fingers with hers, and she knew her instinct was correct. "I fear you might be jealous." She looked up at him through her eyelashes to gauge his response.

His eyes held hers, and Norah hoped the dim light cast from the lamp hid any color that must have come to her cheeks.

"Should I be?" he asked in a low voice.

Her heart soared. A year ago, she wouldn't have thought twice about Ruthann's brother in this way. But his dedication toward helping her with Jeremy, the way he'd protected her on multiple occasions, saved her from Mr. Beck's ardent suit, his kindness toward her parents . . . He'd somehow gone from Jeremy's friend and Ruthann's brother to someone else entirely.

Someone who'd come to mean the world to her.

She shook her head and gave him a shy smile.

The grin he gave her in return could have lit up the night. With his free hand, he softly caressed her cheek. Norah thought her heart might burst from her chest. She could hardly catch her breath as his fingers gently traced her cheekbone. He smelled of whiskey and cigar smoke, but she didn't care.

She stood perfectly still, not wanting to move an inch for fear he'd retract his hand. After all, they were standing outside in full view of anyone who might happen by. Of course, it was late, and the number of decent folks wandering about at such an hour was quite low.

Stuart's eyes, a dark blue in the low light, were fixed on her, and Norah wondered what he was thinking.

"We'll find another way," he said, answering her unspoken question. "Something where I don't have to worry about you for hours on end."

Who knew that knowing she'd been on someone else's mind could make her feel so elated. She reached up and caught his arm. "Stuart?"

He made a sound deep in his throat as his eyes skimmed her face.

"Thank you."

He raised his eyebrows. "For what?"

"Everything." She pressed her cheek into his hand again, and he stepped closer to her. His breath warmed her face and she found herself unable to form a single thought beyond the feel of his hand and noticing the look in his eyes.

He leaned down, his lips barely an inch away from hers, and Norah's eyes closed. He was going to kiss her. And she wouldn't say no. She didn't care one whit that they were standing outside. All she knew was that Stuart Joliet was about to kiss her and she wanted him to so badly it was difficult not to rise up onto her tiptoes to make it happen sooner.

A creak sounded from behind her, and suddenly Stuart's hands were gone. Norah's eyes flew open as the door opened to reveal her father.

"Norah?" Papa's eyes went from her to Stuart. "Stuart? It's late. What are you doing out here?"

Norah tried to speak but the words were caught in her throat. Her head spun as she sought out Stuart.

He was far more composed than she was. He stepped forward, cleared his throat ever so slightly, and said, "I apologize, Mr. Parker. It is indeed late, and Norah didn't want to wake you. I stopped by to wish her good night." He paused. "Good night, Norah."

"Good night," she managed to say.

"Well . . ." Stuart nodded at her father. "I'll be on my way. I'm sorry to have woken you, sir."

He raced down the steps, clearly not wanting to cause Papa to have any other reason to question his presence.

"That was odd," Papa said, watching Stuart as he walked quickly down the street. "Well, come on inside. It's growing cold out here."

Norah nodded. She bent to gather the lamp and glanced out at the street one more time before following Papa inside.

And she hoped next time Stuart tried to kiss her, there would be no interruption.

# Chapter Fourteen

WORK SAT IN PILES ON Stuart's desk, but he had yet to touch any of it. Between thinking about Maddox and his friends' interest in the local freight companies and nearly kissing Norah last night, he couldn't concentrate on anything.

It was nearly noon when Nate arrived. Stuart had traded staring at paperwork for pacing the building and spotted Nate the moment he walked through the door.

"Ruthann sent me to see if you'd like to join us for a quick meal," Nate said. He lowered his voice. "I think she's beside herself with curiosity to learn what you and Norah have uncovered about Jeremy."

It was exactly what Stuart needed to get his worries off his mind. Besides, Nate might have useful insight into why Maddox and the others were so interested in Guelph's and the mines.

He relayed the information to Nate as they walked. "I don't know how it could help with Jeremy—and it may not have anything to do with him at all. But if they're planning something, it might help remove the threat Jeremy received if they're arrested. Or it might provide some way to connect them to the robbery that night."

Nate nodded thoughtfully. "You think Maddox and the others were behind the train robbery?"

"I do. Why else would they threaten Jeremy's family if he fought the charges against him? One of them murdered that railroadman, and they somehow made Jeremy into the guilty party."

"If Jeremy is innocent, why was he at the depot that night?" Nate asked the question that Stuart had posed to Norah.

"I don't know. But if I can figure out what they've got planned for Guelph's, maybe Jeremy will tell us."

Nate was quiet for a moment. They passed the church the Joliets usually attended, and Stuart greeted the minister, who was outside cleaning the church windows. As they walked on, Nate finally spoke up.

"What do you suppose was on the train the night of that robbery? Did they take anything off it?"

Stuart furrowed his brow, thinking. "I don't think so. They'd wrenched a door open, and supposedly the man who was supposed to be guarding the train came to inspect the noise. The gunshot alerted folks nearby, and when the sheriff arrived, he found Jeremy bent over the man he supposedly killed. No one else was around, and not a thing had been taken from the train." He paused. "They must have scattered when the shooting happened and abandoned their plans."

And everyone in town—the sheriff included—assumed Jeremy had done the shooting. It would have been an unbelievable assumption months before, but everyone knew of Jeremy's turn toward the unsavory. It didn't help that he'd been wearing black clothing, had brought a shotgun, and was inches away from the revolver that had killed the fellow he seemed desperate to try to help.

All of the evidence was stacked against him, and everyone thought he was guilty—Stuart included. Everyone except Norah.

"It might be useful to learn what was on that train that they wanted badly enough to kill for it," Nate said.

"You're right." A hundred possibilities ran through Stuart's mind. Most of the freight onboard would have been handled by Joliet's, Guelph's, or one of the smaller shipping companies in town. Which means there would have been receipting for it.

When they reached Nate's studio, they climbed the stairs to the second floor.

Nate was right about Ruthann. She immediately asked for information, and then looked disappointed that he hadn't learned more already. And then just as they were finishing the meal, she began to ask pointed questions about Norah.

"Ruthie." Stuart stood and laid his napkin down on the table. Nate had already excused himself to return to work, and Ruthann avoided his eyes as she cuddled little Caleb. "What exactly are you asking?"

"Oh, nothing in particular." She finally looked up and gave him that sickly sweet smile he knew meant she was after something. "It's only that you've been spending an awful lot of time with Norah, and well . . . she has very flattering things to say about you."

"Oh?" It took every ounce of strength Stuart had not to ask about these supposed *flattering things* Norah discussed.

Ruthann shrugged as she tucked Caleb's blanket around him. "I just want you to know that Norah could do much worse than to find herself being courted by you."

Stuart let out a short laugh. "Thank you, sister. I'll take that as a compliment. Now I must get back to the office."

And he left before his face could betray precisely what he thought about courting Norah. Between Ruthann and Mrs. Parker, it seemed everyone had an opinion on the subject.

He wondered what Norah's opinion was. She hadn't pushed him away last night. It made him hope she was as eager as he'd been for that kiss that hadn't happened.

It made him want to try again as soon as possible.

Thoughts of Norah occupied his mind the entire walk back to the office, but the moment he was through the door, something else took priority.

Stuart went straight to the cabinets in the storage room at the rear of the building. The room kept all sorts of odds and ends—including old paperwork. After several minutes of opening and shutting doors and rifling through stacks of paper, he found what he was looking for.

The receipts dated from early last summer sat at the top of a teetering stack. The fleeting thought that they really needed someone to come back here and organize all of those flew through Stuart's mind before he began sorting through the receipts.

Minutes passed as he moved pages from one stack to another, growing closer and closer to the date of the attempted robbery. And then there it was.

He skimmed through the pages. That specific train had arrived from points west and would have continued on to Pueblo in the morning. Anything that needed to be offloaded and placed on a train to Denver or south to Santa Fe would have been removed when it arrived. And freight intended for points east that had arrived on other trains would have been loaded that evening or early the next morning. Not to mention anything that would have remained on the train for Pueblo or east into Kansas.

Stuart sorted through the receipts, setting aside items marked as received and then sent on to Denver or anywhere that wasn't Pueblo or somewhere else east of there. He looked through what was remaining. A shipment of fruit from a nearby orchard. Coal. A slew of smaller, less expensive sorts of things.

He stepped back, running a hand through his hair. None of it struck him as anything particularly worthy of a late night robbery.

It must not have been something that came through Joliet's, then.

Stuart shuffled the papers together and replaced them in the cabinet, more determined than ever.

There had to be something worth stealing that night, and if he had to visit every freight company in town, he would find it.

# Chapter Fifteen

AS MR. MADDOX LINGERED on her front steps, Norah questioned every decision she'd made that afternoon.

He'd come calling immediately after the noon meal, doffing his hat to Mama and complimenting everything from the parlor furniture to Norah's smile before asking if Norah was free to take a stroll with him along the river.

Dear Mama conveniently offered an excuse—she and Norah were planning to make a visit to Penny Young, the sheriff's wife. Norah thought Mr. Maddox looked sort of pale at the mention of Penny's name, but if he did, he recovered quickly and suggested Norah might postpone her visit until later in the afternoon, when he needed to return to work.

What sort of work Mr. Maddox did, Norah didn't know. He'd never told her, and she suspected he held no respectable job at all.

While every part of her itched to get as far away from him as possible, her mind went back to her conversation with Stuart. Mr. Maddox knew more about what happened that night with Jeremy. She only needed to wheedle it out of him.

*Absolutely not. It's too dangerous.* Stuart's words echoed in her mind as she considered the possibility.

But how dangerous could it be in broad daylight on a public street?

And so she'd gone with him, trying not to draw away when he took her arm. After a bit of small talk, Mr. Maddox turned their conversation again toward Charles's work at Guelph's Freight Company—without Norah needing to steer his thoughts in that direction at all.

He gave away nothing of particular interest, but instead pressed her with questions about Charles. When she told him again that she didn't know much about what Charles's position entailed, he asked if she would introduce him.

*That* was certainly curious. She was hardly about to turn Mr. Maddox's influence on yet another one of her brothers, though. She gave him a noncommittal sort of an answer, telling him she would try but that Charles was awfully busy and she didn't see him much.

Mr. Maddox got a sort of pinched look to his face at that, and Norah could feel the waves of irritation rolling off him. He was silent for a while, and Norah's gaze wandered across the road. And there, just outside the offices of Joliet's Cañon City Shipping and Freight, was Stuart.

She couldn't see his expression from her place across the road, but given the way he turned on his heel and stalked back inside, she was certain he was none too happy about her choice of company. She felt a twinge of guilt, doing this without mentioning it to him, specifically when he'd expressed such concern over her spending time with Mr. Maddox.

But she was going about it in a safe way. And Stuart ought to know her well enough to trust her by now.

*Let him stew.* He'd forgive her when she told him about Mr. Maddox's single-minded focus on Guelph's. He and his friends were plotting something. It was painfully obvious, and Mr. Maddox clearly thought her too simple-minded to see that.

They were nearly back to her house when Mr. Maddox spoke the words that had chilled Norah to her very core.

"I've been thinking about Jeremy," he said. "Have you been to visit him?"

Norah nearly froze. She had to force her feet to continue moving toward the steps that led to her front door. He was waiting for her answer, and if she couldn't formulate one quickly, he'd know something was wrong.

And that wouldn't bode well for Jeremy, her family, or herself.

"Why, no, I haven't." She'd managed to choke out the words as she climbed the steps. Thankfully he was at her back, unable to see her expression as she spoke. "Our family doesn't speak with him after what he did. I'm sure you understand." Composing herself, she'd turned to face him.

He seemed to stare right through her to her very soul as she tried to breathe normally. Why had she thought this was a good idea? She was half a second away from Mr. Maddox guessing her words were a lie.

"I understand," he finally said. "And I think it wise." Nothing in the way he smiled at her gave her any hint he didn't believe her.

Somewhat lightheaded, Norah grabbed hold of the doorknob to steady herself—and to silently convey she was ready to end their afternoon.

Thankfully, Mr. Maddox took the hint. He also took her free hand, bent over it, and kissed it.

Norah thought she might be ill. She managed not to yank her hand away. Even through her glove, she could feel his lips, and she shuddered inside.

He bid her good afternoon, and she slipped inside the door and made her way immediately to the parlor to sink into a chair.

How nice it was to be home! She would never take this comforting, simple place for granted again. Its sturdy four walls kept Mr. Maddox outside, and for that, Norah could wish for nothing better.

"Norah?" Mama appeared in the doorway. "I'm glad to see you home. Did Mr. Maddox leave?"

Norah nodded, and Mama pressed a hand to her heart as her shoulders sunk in clear relief.

"I must confess—again—that I don't like the man at all. I wish you wouldn't entertain his interest in you," Mama said.

"Oh, I'm not. I promise that was the last time I'll spend another moment with Mr. Maddox. I have no interest in him whatsoever," Norah replied emphatically.

"I'm glad to hear it. I think Stuart is much more suited to you. He's a gentleman and he comes from a good family. And—"

Norah stood suddenly, cutting off Mama's words. *Stuart.* She needed to see him immediately. Not just to tell him what she'd learned, but also to assuage any hurt feelings he might have about seeing her with Mr. Maddox.

"Is everything all right?" Mama looked at her in concern.

"It's fine. I . . . need to see Stuart." She was already making her way toward the door.

"Right now? Norah, it's hardly seemly for a woman to go chasing after a man—"

"Mama!" Norah whirled around. "I am not *chasing* after him. I'm simply paying him a visit."

"Yes, but he'll think you too interested, and that always lessens a man's attraction to a lady."

Norah's impatience threatened to bubble over into her words. She took a deep breath and tamped it down. Mama only wanted the best for her, and this was her way of showing it. Norah wouldn't let her annoyance get the best of her and hurt Mama's feelings. "This is not about courting, I promise. Stuart is an old friend, and there is something I must tell him right away."

"Are you certain it can't wait?" Mama still looked concerned as she twisted her hands in front of her.

"I am. I'll be home in time to help you with supper." Norah didn't wait for a response. She shut the door firmly behind her, glanced down the road to ensure Mr. Maddox wasn't lingering, and retied the ribbons of her hat while she raced down the steps.

She made it to Stuart's office so quickly she was nearly out of breath. Catching hold of the doorknob, she gave herself a moment to breathe and smooth down her skirts before pushing the door open.

If Mr. Joliet was surprised to see her, he had the manners not to show it. Standing near the desk of a clerk, he pointed her toward Stuart's office. As she moved down the hallway, which smelled of wood and importance, she realized she hadn't been in here in years. The last time, she'd been tagging along with Jeremy.

Stuart's door was open, and she found him staring at nothing with his head between his hands. He jerked when he saw her and jumped up.

"Norah," he said curtly.

Norah stopped herself from rolling her eyes at his obvious irritation. She might as well get immediately to the point. "Please don't act as if you're jealous. I merely had the opportunity to learn more about Mr. Maddox, and so I took it."

Stuart clenched his jaw. He'd come around the side of his desk, and now his hand gripped the edge of it. "I am *not* jealous. I'm frustrated that I told you to stay away from him because of the danger, and yet you threw that back in my face by openly placing yourself right in the lion's den."

Norah pressed her lips together. Guilt licked at her insides. He really did only want the best for her. "I'm sorry I made you worry."

"But not for choosing to endanger both yourself and your family? What if you said something that led Maddox to believe Jeremy's spoken to you?"

Norah straightened her shoulders. "You can trust me to do better than that. In fact, he asked me if I'd visited Jeremy, and he believed me when I told him my family didn't speak to my brother."

Now it was Stuart's turn to look chagrined. "I do trust you," he said quietly. "But I worry about you. If anything happened, Norah, I . . ."

He stepped forward then, his eyes holding her gaze.

"Yes?" she prodded. She gripped her skirts to hide her shaking hands. Surely he wouldn't try to kiss her again now, not in this office when anyone—even his own father—could come strolling down the hallway.

As if he read her mind, Stuart looked toward the empty hallway before turning his attention back to her. "I would blame myself entirely. And I would never be able to forgive myself."

Norah swallowed as he gazed at her with such an intensity in his eyes. *Kiss me now*, she thought.

But it wasn't to be, as Mr. Joliet called Stuart's name from somewhere down the hall. Heaving a sigh, Stuart stepped back. "I didn't tell you that I searched through our old receipts, trying to determine what was on the train that night. I found nothing, but it may have been something one of the other companies has record of."

Norah nodded, trying to force her thoughts back from the precipice. "Mr. Maddox asked to meet Charles. He was clearly annoyed when I indicated that might be difficult."

Stuart nodded. "He's very interested in Guelph's. Do you suppose we could ask Charles to look through their receipts?"

"It would be difficult to do so without giving away that we've visited Jeremy." She paused. "Let me think about it. There may be a way we can get in there to see them ourselves."

"Stuart!" Mr. Joliet's voice bellowed down the hallway again.

"Come, I'll walk you out."

Norah took Stuart's arm, grateful for the distraction of a problem to solve.

Else she'd be among the clouds the rest of the evening, imagining the kiss that still had yet to come.

# Chapter Sixteen

"I DON'T KNOW HOW LONG I can keep Charles talking about advertising," Stuart said as he and Norah walked toward Guelph's the next day.

"Perhaps you can pose something unbelievable—going in together on advertising or something like that. Anything to keep him talking and give me enough time to sort through their old receipts." Norah looked more determined than Stuart had ever seen her.

And he decided that was something he liked very much about her. She wasn't one to give in easily. And she was more loyal than any man he'd ever met. She would do anything and everything to have Jeremy released from prison.

"All right," Stuart replied. "I'll try and persuade him to join me at the diner. That should give you plenty of time."

They turned the corner, and Guelph's came into view—along with Nate, who was hurrying along the sidewalk as if being chased by ghosts.

Stuart paused, Norah at his side, as he watched his friend. Nate was one who took things slowly. Who thought before speaking, and who always allowed himself plenty of time to arrive when expected somewhere. Rushing along the street was not normal for Nate.

Which meant there was a problem.

Praying it was not Ruthann, Stuart started forward again. "Something's wrong." He spoke quietly so only Norah could hear.

She looked up at him in alarm, but before he could say anything else, Nate had reached them.

"You need to come with me, both of you," he said in a low voice. "Right now."

Stuart didn't hesitate. He and Norah fell into step beside Nate as he led them back the way they'd come—toward his studio and second floor home.

"What happened? Is it Ruthann?" A hundred scenarios rushed through Stuart's head, each one worse than the last.

Nate shook his head, and Stuart exhaled in relief.

"Then what is it?" Norah asked, her face troubled.

Nate gave them both a look that clearly said he wouldn't speak about it. Thankfully, it wasn't far to the photography studio, else Stuart's imagination would have concocted six fires, a gang of outlaws, and a band of renegade Indians all descending upon the studio's door.

Once they were safely inside with the door shut and locked behind them, Nate led the way to the rear of the room. The curtains on the windows were shut, which was odd for this time of day. After all, Nate's photographs were better with ample light.

But when a figure stepped out from inside Nate's darkroom, Stuart knew why the door was locked and the windows were shut.

"Jeremy." Norah breathed his name, throwing a hand over her mouth before bursting forward and embracing him in a bone-crushing hug.

"Did you have to go to the Parkers'?" Ruthann asked from where she stood near the darkroom door.

Nate shook his head. "By chance I found them both just a few blocks away."

Stuart looked from Nate to his sister to where Norah still embraced her brother. "Will someone explain what's happening here? How is Jeremy— Why is Jeremy—?"

Norah stepped back from her brother, her face lit in the happiest smile Stuart had seen in a long time.

"I'm hoping he'll tell us now that you're here," Nate said. He stood perfectly straight, as if expecting prison guards to come bursting in through the door at any moment.

"I escaped," Jeremy said. "While we were out working the quarry."

Stuart's heart sunk. It was the worst thing he could have done. How were they supposed to prove his innocence when he ran off? It made him look untrustworthy and—frankly—guilty.

"How?" Norah asked, her eyes wide.

"It's easy enough if you know what to look for. Happens more often than the prison lets on," Jeremy said.

Nate narrowed his eyes. "Because most of the time they catch the prisoners before the town can get its feathers ruffled. Which means they're out there looking for you right now."

Jeremy looked at him, his eyes serious. "I know. And the last thing I want is to get any of you into trouble, but I had to come." He paused, looking at each of them in turn. "You need to leave town. All of you. Our parents and Charles and Mary too," he said to Norah.

"I don't understand." Nate crossed his arms. "Why?"

The expression on Jeremy's face had gone pale and fearful. And Stuart knew.

"They found out," Stuart said, his voice hollow. "Maddox, Chase, all of them. How?"

"I don't know," Jeremy said. "I suspect they paid someone who paid the guard who was in the room with us. That's all I can think of. But it doesn't matter, because Maddox knows I've talked, and he knows what you're doing. You have to *go*."

Norah nodded. "All right. We'll run home and then come back here for you."

Jeremy shook his head. "I'm not going with you. Maddox will be angry when he discovers you've all left. He can take his frustrations out on me."

"No!" Norah grabbed his arm, clearly horrified at the suggestion while Ruthann wrapped a comforting arm around Norah's shoulders.

Stuart glanced at Nate, trying to discern what he thought about all of this.

"*If* we were to leave—" Stuart started, but a pounding at the front door interrupted him.

"Harper! You in there? Open the door!" Sheriff Young's voice was urgent and commanding.

Norah's eyes widened. "You have to hide, Jeremy. Now!"

Jeremy shook his head. "I did what I came here to do. I'm going to let them take me back. You should all go upstairs, pretend you never saw me. I'll tell them I snuck in."

"No." Nate shook his head. "I'm not letting all of this fall on you. I'll tell them you heard that Ruthann had fallen ill, and you wished to help."

The pounding on the door came again. "Harper! Open up!"

Jeremy tried to protest, but Nate remained resolute. Ruthann opened the door to the darkroom and motioned for Stuart and Norah to go inside. Norah hesitated, and then slipped in. Stuart followed her and held open the door for Ruthann.

"No," she said softly. "If Nate remains out here, my place is with him. Norah, Caleb is upstairs sleeping. If anything happens . . . will you take him with you? Bring him to my mother's. I'll come for him as soon as I can."

Norah nodded as Stuart swore under his breath.

"Ruthann, no. Nate, tell her—" But he didn't finish the sentence. The door cracked under a heavy thud.

"Jeremy!" Stuart whispered just before another thud sounded. "What was on the train that night?"

Jeremy wrinkled his forehead and then nodded in understanding. "Nothing. I told Maddox there was a large shipment of jewelry going to a shop in California, but I'd made it up."

"Why? What were you doing there that night?" Stuart asked.

But Jeremy didn't answer. The front door crashed open and Ruthann shoved the darkroom door closed.

"There he is!" an unfamiliar voice called across the room.

Norah choked back a sob, and Stuart reached for her in the dark, drawing her close to him. She buried her face in his chest and he held her to him as he listened to the commotion outside.

"There's no need for force," Nate said. "He isn't fighting you, and he isn't armed."

Sheriff Young echoed Nate's request, clearly irritated with whomever had come from the prison to find Jeremy. Norah's fingers dug into Stuart's arms, and he rubbed a circle on her back as he listened.

"Are these the people responsible for hiding him here?" a gruff voice asked.

"I'm sure—" Sheriff Young began, but Jeremy interrupted.

"They've done nothing wrong. I snuck in myself. I didn't think anyone was here," Jeremy said.

"And yet here they are, not opening the door when asked and not turning you out. Sheriff, I demand you place these people under arrest."

Stuart scowled into the darkness as Nate attempted to tell the story he'd concocted about Jeremy believing Ruthann was gravely ill.

But none of it made a bit of difference, because with an apology in hand, Sheriff Young placed Nate under arrest.

When the man from the prison insisted Ruthann be taken off to jail too, the sheriff's patience ended entirely. "You've got what you wanted. I'm not taking the lady to a jail cell."

"Thank you, Sheriff," Ruthann said softly. "But I insist on accompanying you. I'd like to see after my husband."

There was some scuffling, and then finally the door shut. The silence somehow seemed louder than the commotion that had preceded it.

"They've left," Stuart whispered, still not entirely trusting the situation. He loosened his grip on Norah and, very carefully, cracked the door open. Not a soul remained in the studio.

"What do we do now?" Norah asked as she stepped out.

Stuart went to the broken front door, assessing how much effort it would take to fix. He wasn't about to leave Ruthann and her child in a home with a door that didn't shut all the way, much less lock. "We fix this door. And then we figure out why Jeremy was at the depot the night of the robbery."

# Chapter Seventeen

NORAH FETCHED BABY Caleb from his cradle upstairs while Stuart pieced wood together to temporarily fix the door. Caleb only fussed a little, and she held him close and whispered words of comfort in his ear.

"That should do," Stuart said, stepping back from the door. He set the hammer down and tested the door. "Are you ready?"

Norah nodded. Tucking Caleb against her, she followed Stuart outside. He kept close to her, and neither of them spoke on the way to the Joliets' home. Norah had never felt so fearful walking along the street in her own little town, but now it seemed as if Mr. Maddox or any number of his friends could leap out from a doorway or be waiting just around a corner.

Her shoulders sunk with relief when she stepped inside the home Stuart shared with his parents. Mr. Joliet, thankfully, had just arrived home. While Stuart quickly explained the situation, Norah handed the baby to Mrs. Joliet.

"You ought to go somewhere safer," Stuart urged. "To a neighbor's, perhaps."

"Absolutely not," Mr. Joliet said in a way that made him sound exactly like Stuart. "I'll keep a pistol nearby and lock the doors, but we aren't leaving our home."

Stuart didn't attempt to dissuade him. "I need to warn Norah's parents and her brother."

"You'll wait here with us, dear," Mrs. Joliet said, reaching out to clasp Norah's hand. Norah couldn't help but admire her. Her fear was evident in her eyes, but she stood strong and determined, not conveying an ounce of worry in her mannerisms.

Norah nodded, and with a quick squeeze of her hand, Stuart was gone. Mr. and Mrs. Joliet exchanged a look but said nothing. They sat in the parlor, Mr. Joliet attempting to read, and his wife fussing over the baby, while Norah could concentrate on nothing except her own worries. She prayed for Stuart's and her family's safety, for Jeremy, for Nate and Ruthann, over and over until the words ran together in her head. And then she thought on Jeremy's last words to them before they'd closed the door to the darkroom.

There had been nothing for Maddox and his men to steal. Jeremy had made it up. But why?

Outside, the sun had begun to set, and just as she thought she'd burst if she had to wait a moment longer, Stuart returned.

"Oh, thank goodness!" Mrs. Joliet had laid Caleb down to sleep a while ago, and now she embraced her son as if she'd never let him go again. It took every bit of strength Norah had not to go rushing to Stuart and throwing her own arms around him.

"I haven't seen to Ruthann and Nate yet," Stuart said when she finally let him go. "I'll bring her back here."

"I'm going with you." Norah was already reaching for her wrap.

Stuart shook his head. "I want you to stay here," he said at the same time Mrs. Joliet insisted the same thing.

"No!" Norah said a little more forcefully than she'd intended. Securing the wrap over her shoulders, she took a deep breath and added, "I can't sit here doing nothing. Besides, if something were to happen . . . I could go for help."

Stuart glanced at the door. Time was ticking by—and Stuart wasn't about to waste precious moments arguing with her.

"I can help," she added.

He caught her eyes, and she held his gaze. Finally, he nodded. "Let's go."

"Wait." Mr. Joliet took one of his pistols and handed it to Stuart. "I've got the shotgun here."

Norah felt a hand on her arm. When she turned, she found Mrs. Joliet holding out the second pistol. "Don't hesitate if anyone tries to hurt you," she said.

Norah nodded and slid the weapon into her dress pocket. She didn't have the slightest idea how to use it, but perhaps its simple presence would be enough.

"Come back here as soon as you can with Ruthann," Mrs. Joliet said as they left, her hand lingering on Stuart's arm."

"We will. I promise," Stuart replied.

He took up her arm, just as he would if they were taking a relaxing evening stroll, but there was nothing leisurely about this walk.

"While you were gone," Norah said through short breaths as they walked quickly down the road. "I thought about why Jeremy would have lied to Mr. Maddox about a valuable shipment on that train. He must have known Mr. Maddox would want to steal it. But why go through all that trouble?"

"They must have done it before. Maddox and his men. And they were planning to do it again," Stuart added as he looked back and forth across the street and then behind them. "It's the only reason I can figure for him to do that."

"He wanted to prevent an actual robbery from happening at the depot. So he fed them false information and pretended to go along with them." Norah's mind spun with the new information. Her breath caught. "That means he was never a friend of Maddox's. All those nights he spent at one saloon or another . . . all the money he lost gambling . . ."

"It was all for show. All to convince Maddox and the others that he was their friend," Stuart finished for her. He shook his head. "I had no idea."

"Jeremy went to prison, and now Mr. Maddox is preparing to do this all over again with some shipment Guelph's is coordinating with one of the mines." Norah ran it all through her head again. There was something that didn't make sense. Something that . . .

"Stuart! Why would Jeremy go through all that trouble and not have anyone there to catch Maddox and the others in the act?"

"Sheriff Young," Stuart said. "He was the first to arrive, wasn't he?"

Norah nodded. That was what she'd heard.

"What if . . ." Stuart gazed out into the growing darkness. Norah was quiet as he thought.

"What if Jeremy had alerted the sheriff? I'd heard it was the gunshot that had drawn him to the depot, but perhaps he was already set to go there because Jeremy had told him?" Stuart looked to her for her reaction.

"Yes . . ." Norah pinched her lips together, thinking. "But wouldn't he have said as much at the trial? I would have thought we'd have heard about that."

"Unless Jeremy alerted him anonymously. If Sheriff Young had no idea who had informed him to keep an eye on the depot that night, he would have no way of knowing Jeremy was innocent. And then he arrived and found—"

"Only Jeremy," Norah finished for him.

Jeremy must have feared Mr. Maddox and the others learning he had betrayed them, so he'd kept the information he'd given to the sheriff anonymous. It was the only explanation. And if Sheriff Young had only received vague information that something was happening at the depot that night, that wouldn't have been news enough to make the papers. Neither Norah nor Stuart would have had any way of knowing a minute detail such as that without having attended Jeremy's trial.

"We need to speak to the sheriff," Stuart said. "Maybe Jeremy left some clue as to his identity when he alerted Young. Something Young wouldn't notice, but maybe you or I would."

For the first time that night, hope pushed away the fear that had lodged itself inside Norah. All they needed was one little bit of proof. One tiny shred of evidence, and Jeremy could be free.

And Mr. Maddox would be out of their lives for good.

# Chapter Eighteen

IT WAS FULLY DARK BY the time they reached the sheriff's office and jail. Stuart knocked, but there was no answer. Young had likely gone upstairs for supper. Heart sinking, he tried the door, expecting to find it locked.

But the knob turned under his hand, and the door opened to reveal an empty office.

"Hello? Sheriff?" Stuart called as they stepped inside.

"He left a lamp." Norah pointed at the lamp burning on the desk.

Stuart narrowed his eyes. Young wouldn't do something so dangerous as to leave a lamp burning while he went upstairs to eat. Besides, he'd need the light to see to go up the stairs.

Something didn't feel quite right.

Placing his finger to his lips to let Norah know to remain quiet, he stepped farther into the room. The silence thudded in his ears, louder than a train's whistle.

Norah pointed to the ceiling and mouthed, "Upstairs?"

It was possible. But first they needed to check on Nate—and Ruthann, if she was down here. He gestured at the door that led to the town's jail cells, before drawing his father's pistol just in case trouble waited on the other side.

Norah fell into step behind him, and silently, they crossed the room. Stuart reached out with his free hand for the door. It creaked open to a space lit with another lamp.

And four men standing with guns aiming right at him.

"HAND IT OVER, JOLIET," Maddox said. He was leaning lazily against a cell that held Nate and Ruthann. The cell next to that one contained Sheriff Young, Mrs. Young, and one of the sheriff's deputies, Harry Caldwell.

Maddox held out a hand, waiting for Stuart to hand over his pistol. Stuart glanced behind him, hoping Norah had backed out and run away.

But of course she hadn't. She stood here with her chin tilted upward as if a passel of men with guns pointed at them didn't unnerve her at all.

Stuart turned back to the men in front of them. Even if he fired and hit Maddox, the others would fire at him right away. If he tried to back out, they'd shoot.

He and Norah were trapped here, just as the sheriff and the others had been. Stuart had played right into Maddox's hands, and now Maddox had half the people he wished to see dead in one place.

He had no other choice. Stuart drew in a breath before turning the pistol around in his hand and placing it in Maddox's.

"Thank you," Maddox said as if Stuart had handed him a slice of pie or a handful of coins. "Miss Parker, would you be so kind as to step into the room?"

Stuart reached for her arm as she stopped beside him. If Maddox attempted to do so much as reach for her hand, no amount of pistols pointed at him would stop Stuart from leaping at Maddox to knock him to the ground.

"Well, isn't this convenient?" Maddox said, letting his revolver dangle from his hand as if he weren't the slightest bit worried about Stuart and Norah escaping.

"Let's get this over with," Sid Chase said from his place near the wall. His red hair glowed in the lamplight, and he hadn't lowered his gun even an inch.

Maddox held up a hand. "Not yet. We need Miss Parker." He narrowed his eyes at Stuart. "And Mrs. Harper."

*Ruthann*. Stuart's heart hammered against his chest. "Why?"

A slow, vicious smile traced its way across Maddox's face. "I'm assuming you had plenty of time to pay a visit to your family and to Miss Parker's. The only way we'll get in quietly is with a little help from the ladies."

Stuart clenched his free hand into a fist at his side. "They have nothing to do with this. And for that matter, neither does anyone else you've got in those cells. Let them go and you can have me."

Maddox laughed, and Chase joined in. The other two men looked just as amused, and Stuart wished he could take each one of them on.

"You all know too much, and that's a liability to us," Maddox said, his mirth disappearing as quick as it had arrived.

"And so your plan is to shoot every of one us?" Sheriff Young scowled at Maddox.

Maddox didn't answer. It didn't matter, though, because when Stuart glanced at the sheriff, it was clear he knew the answer too.

They would all die right here, unless he or Norah could come up with something to end this. And with just the two of them up against four armed men, it felt like a hopeless situation.

"Why are you here?" Stuart asked. If he kept Maddox talking, it would create more time for him to think of a plan. "After that robbery went wrong, and you managed to get Jeremy Parker convicted, why would you stay?"

Maddox cast an irritated glance at him.

"Jeremy tricked him," Norah said, and Stuart could have kissed her right then and there for apparently understanding what he was doing. "He told Mr. Maddox about a false shipment—something valuable he knew Mr. Maddox and these men couldn't resist. And then he found a way to alert Sheriff Young that something was going to happen that night. Except—"

"I never knew it was Parker." Sheriff Young frowned. "It was an anonymous note, sent to me that afternoon. If I'd known . . ."

There was no need to finish the sentence.

"Enough." Maddox's voice cut through the silence. "Parker was a liability, and I made sure he's exactly where he should be. He won't be in my way again. Chase, you'll take Mrs. Harper and go to her parents' home. Rodriguez and I will accompany Miss Parker to her home and her brother's." That left the last man, the tall blond fellow Stuart remembered from the saloon, to remain at the sheriff's office with everyone else. Clearly Maddox thought the ladies would be more compliant if they left here while everyone else was still alive.

But Stuart wouldn't put it past Maddox to quietly order the man staying here to shoot them all the second Maddox and the others had left with Ruthann and Norah.

Stuart refused to let that happen. Not so long as he still drew breath.

As Maddox discussed specifics with the other men, Stuart forced himself to think. There were more of them than there were of Maddox's men. If only they could somehow get the others out of the cells . . .

Chase held the keys. Stuart could see them dangling from his trousers pocket. He'd need to use them to release Ruthann—and to lock up Stuart. There might be an opportunity then . . . *If* Stuart could act quickly enough.

And if he didn't think too much on how it would likely end with one of those men shooting him.

It would be worth it if Nate or Ruthann could get out and toss the keys to the sheriff.

Stuart clenched and unclenched his fist, trying to quell the fear that rose alongside his growing courage. He glanced at Norah, wanting to memorize every last line and plain of her face, and the feel of her skin under his hand. If he didn't survive, he would die with her image emblazoned in his mind. He only wished he could give her that kiss that was so long promised.

But in the middle of all that reminiscing and wishing and memorizing, the look on Norah's face changed.

The fear that tightened her mouth vanished, she slipped her arm from Stuart's hand, and her gaze focused on Maddox.

Then she reached down and, from her dress pocket, she withdrew a pistol.

# Chapter Nineteen

THE TIGHTER SHE HELD onto the pistol, the more her fear vanished.

The revolver that Mrs. Joliet had slipped into her hand before she and Stuart had left his parents' home was heavy, but Norah barely noticed. She aimed it right at Mr. Maddox—and she prayed she was holding it correctly.

It took a moment for him to notice, but Stuart certainly had. She didn't dare look at him, but she could see him step off to the side out of the corner of her eye. She didn't know what he was doing, and she didn't have time to guess.

Maddox's men raised their guns again, but Maddox gestured for them to lower their arms. "Miss Parker," he said in the most condescending voice Norah had ever heard. "Aiming a pistol doesn't suit you. Why don't you set it down?"

She didn't speak—if she did, she was afraid her voice would shake and betray the confidence she was trying so hard to project.

*Back away*, she thought. *Give up now.*

But it was a futile wish. Mr. Maddox just looked at her with a smile that resembled the one a father might give to a small child who'd broken a dish.

"The lady looks determined," Sheriff Young. "I wouldn't want to be in your place."

"Shut your mouth, Sheriff. When I want your commentary, I'll ask for it," Maddox snapped.

His patience had worn thin, despite the tight smile he gave Norah again. "Put the pistol *down*, Miss Parker."

She held steady, praying to God that she wouldn't be forced to use it. She had a vague notion of how it worked, but she didn't care to test her knowledge.

"You're making me lose my temper," Maddox said through clenched teeth. "I don't want to have to come over there and wrestle it from your hands."

"Do it," Norah said, speaking before she could think too long on what she was saying.

Ruthann gasped, but Norah didn't take her eyes from Mr. Maddox.

He took a step forward, but still she didn't make a move.

"Let me shoot her now and get it over with," one of the other men said.

Norah's stomach heaved, but she drew in a breath. If she'd guessed correctly, Maddox wouldn't allow it.

"No," he said, holding up a hand. "We need her." He paused a moment. "But we don't need Mr. Joliet."

*Stuart*. Norah couldn't help it then. She glanced at Stuart—but he was no longer beside her. Instead, while the men were preoccupied with Norah, he'd slipped slowly off to the side of the room, and then down the wall, until he was steps away from the red-haired man Mr. Maddox had referred to as Chase.

The others seemed to notice him at the same time. Biting her lip, Norah did the one thing she'd hoped she wouldn't have to do.

Hoping she remembered seeing it done correctly before, she pulled the hammer down—and then she squeezed the trigger.

The sound was deafening, and Norah felt herself scream as the pistol seemed to jump in her hands.

Chaos erupted. Stuart threw himself at Chase. Maddox lunged toward Norah. She quickly moved backward, out of his grasp, and was able to narrow her thoughts just enough to aim the pistol at him again. He scowled at her, and with a snarl of disgust, threw up his hands and backed away.

"Shoot her!" he yelled as he disappeared behind the tall blond man who'd been closest to the cells.

But no one obeyed him. The short, blemished man was trying to pull Stuart away from Chase, while the blond man followed their progress with his revolver pointed at the knot of the three men.

Suddenly, a clinking sound skittered across the floor. Norah looked down.

There, right at her feet, were the keys to the cells.

She bent down, careful not to lower the pistol, and scooped them up.

"Norah!" Ruthann called over the shouts of the men. She pointed to the cell closest to Norah—the one that held the sheriff, Deputy Caldwell, and Penny Young.

Norah didn't pause to think. She tossed the keys in their direction. They slipped through the bars and landed inside. Sheriff Young wasted no time unlocking the cell.

"They've got the keys!" The creaking sound of the lock had alerted the taller man. He swung around and aimed his pistol at the sheriff—but it was too late.

Sheriff Young tossed the keys to his wife before barreling into the man, sending him flying against the wall, just on the opposite side of Maddox.

Deputy Caldwell followed right behind the sheriff and aimed himself at Maddox just as Maddox yanked his revolver from his holster again.

With a glance at Norah, Maddox aimed the gun at Stuart, who had Chase pinned to the ground.

"No!" Norah shouted. "Stuart!"

Time seemed to slow. The deputy lunged at Maddox—but it was too late.

The shot rang out just half a second before Deputy Caldwell reached Maddox. Maddox went down hard, but Norah barely saw him. Her eyes were on Stuart, who'd slipped off to the side of Chase.

A bloom of red began to spread across his shirt where his coat had fallen away.

He'd been shot.

# Chapter Twenty

THE PAIN WAS FIRE-HOT, spreading quickly across his side. Stuart tried to sit up, but his head spun. All he could do was fall backward onto the floor.

Chase was gone. What had happened to him? Stuart tried to clear his head, but it was impossible to think because of the fire.

*No.*

He'd been prepared to die. But now he refused to let it happen.

Norah fell to the floor beside him, her hands on his, and then tugging at his shirt. Then she was pressing something hard against his side.

Stuart sucked in a gasp of pain and tried not to swear, not in front of Norah.

"Go ahead," she said. "Say anything you like. Just stay awake. Stay here with me." Her hand reached for his and squeezed.

Stuart was only vaguely aware of everyone around him. When he tried to turn his head, the pain intensified.

"It's all right. We're safe now," Norah said. "You threw those keys, and I got them to the sheriff. It's over. They're putting Maddox and those other men in the cells." She paused, and when she spoke again, her voice cracked. "You saved us, Stuart. You saved all of us."

"No," he croaked. "You . . ."

She laughed, tremulous but sweet all the same. He'd thought before that he could listen to that laugh all his life. If he were bound for heaven now, he only hoped it would be filled with the sound of Norah's laughter.

"I didn't shoot anything save for the wall," she said. "All I did was pretend I could. You're the one who ended this."

He wanted to protest, to tell her she was the bravest woman he'd ever known, but the doctor arrived just then and she was showing him where Stuart had been shot.

Doc Wallen pulled away the cloth Norah had pressed against Stuart's side and peeled back his shirt. He was silent for a few moments while he examined the wound.

"There's a lot of blood," he finally said, looking at Stuart. "But the good news is that it went through clean. And it doesn't appear to have hit anything vital."

"Are you certain?" Ruthann's voice sounded from Stuart's other side. He turned his head just a little, ignoring the pain, to see his sister kneeling beside him, Mrs. Young at her side.

"As certain as the sun sets." Doc Wallen gave him a fatherly smile. "You'll live, son. It'll hurt for a time, but I can get you stitched up and it won't be long before you're back to normal."

Stuart wasn't entirely sure how something less than lethal could hurt so badly, but both Norah and Ruthann thanked the doctor up and down and sideways, so he must be telling the truth.

Doc Wallen stood. "If a few of you boys can carry him to my office, I'll get it taken care of."

Before Stuart could react, Nate and Deputy Caldwell had lifted him and began carrying him toward the door.

"Please be careful," Norah called.

"Norah," Mrs. Young said from somewhere behind Stuart. "Why don't you and Ruthann come upstairs for a while? You must be exhausted."

"Thank you, Penny, but I must go with Stuart." Norah paused. "I can't leave him."

Her words were like a balm to the searing pain that had overtaken him as Nate and the deputy carried him through the sheriff's office. He was growing light-headed again, and he felt too tired to keep his eyes open.

He closed them, smiling at the thought of Norah's concern for him.

STUART AWOKE TO A DULL throbbing in his side and a very uncomfortable bed under his back. It was mostly dark in the room, but a low lamp cast the slightest light. It took him a moment to realize where he was—Doc Wallen's office—and to remember why he was there.

He shifted and grit his teeth together as that dull pain became sharper.

"Stuart?" Norah's soft voice came from somewhere across the room. In half a moment, she was by his bedside. "You're awake."

"I'm beginning to wish I wasn't." Maybe if he remained perfectly still, that knife-like feeling in his side would diminish to a low ache again.

Norah brushed his hair from his face, and then paused. She went to pull her hand away as if she thought the gesture wouldn't be welcome.

Stuart reached out and grabbed her hand, ignoring the pain from his side that protested at such movement. Norah smiled at him and sunk onto the edge of the bed, her hand still in his.

"Does it hurt much?" she asked.

"Not anymore," he lied.

She shook her head. "I don't believe you, but I'm glad you can still make a joke."

"Maddox?"

"In a cell, along with the others."

"Good."

"What time is it?" he asked, not daring to turn his head to find a clock.

"Nearly two in the morning. And don't you dare tell me to go home. Doc Wallen is asleep in the next room. He was wonderful, convincing Mama and Papa that you needed a nurse by your side tonight."

Stuart didn't believe such a thing was entirely necessary, and he suspected Norah knew it too. Yet neither one of them was about to complain.

"Sheriff Young came by earlier, while you were asleep. He'd searched through his things and found that note he'd received before the robbery. He brought it here to show me, and I identified Jeremy's handwriting. He's going to get a sample of Jeremy's writing and present it to the judge. And he'll tell him what Mr. Maddox shared with us back at the jail. With any luck, the case will be reopened—"

"And Jeremy will be freed," Stuart finished for her.

"Yes." She gave him such a bright smile that it was hard to believe that anything bad had ever happened.

Looking at her now, it was difficult to imagine a time in which he'd seen her only as Ruthann's friend, or Jeremy's irritating little sister. It seemed impossible, now that he'd gotten to know Norah. To see her bravery, her loyalty, her belief in the truth, and the way she loved those around her so fiercely that she would never abandon them.

"Norah," he said, unable to hold it inside any longer. "There is something I must tell you."

Her eyes widened, and he wondered if she anticipated what he would say. If maybe she *hoped* for it. Because if she didn't feel the same way about him, Stuart didn't know what he would do next.

"Yes?" she said, her voice a bit breathless.

Saying the words out loud required more courage than throwing himself into danger back at the jail. He wanted to laugh at the thought—that somehow confessing his feelings for Norah was more terrifying than four men pointing guns at him.

She was looking at him intently now, waiting.

*Say it.*

"I love you."

# Chapter Twenty-one

THE JOY THAT BUBBLED up from inside Norah at hearing those three simple words was unlike anything else she'd ever experienced.

Stuart *loved* her.

And suddenly, everything was right in the world. Jeremy would be free. Her family would be together again and happy.

And Stuart . . .

She dropped his hand and leaned over to embrace him.

He laughed a little in her ear, and then sucked in a breath as his hand rested on her back.

Norah froze and then rose slowly so she could see him. "Have I hurt you?"

"Never." He watched her with such light in his eyes that if someone had told Norah it was the middle of the day, she would have believed it.

She looked at him a moment, tracing every feature of his face. "I love you too, Stuart," she finally said.

He smiled then. "If I weren't stuck here in this bed, I'd pick you up and swing you around."

Norah laughed. Her hand found his face, tracing gentle fingers across his cheek and down his jaw. "I was so afraid that I was going to lose you."

"I'm here," he whispered. "And I'll never leave you."

Norah swallowed. "Thank you for believing me. For believing *in* me."

"Always."

"I suppose now you'll ask me to dance at the church social again?" She gave him a grin.

"Well . . . I was hoping I might have every dance from now on." His eyes held hers, and Norah's heart skipped forward.

"Would you marry me, Norah Parker? I can't promise to be perfect, and I tend to be a bit overbearing, but I will be yours until the end. I'll devote myself to you, and to our family if we're so blessed." Stuart watched her with the most earnest expression.

Norah had been wrong. *This* was the happiest she'd ever felt. "Yes. Yes, yes, I will!" She couldn't say the words fast enough.

Stuart gave her a broad grin. "Now will you do me one more favor?"

"You'd like me to play you a tune on the piano? I know an entire selection I like to call 'Buzzing Insects.'" She bit her lip, trying to contain the laughter that threatened to bubble up.

"Oh, please, no," Stuart said with a feigned expression of pain. "I was hoping you might lean down here and kiss me. Considering I fear I'd tear open stitches if I were to sit up and—"

He didn't need to say another word, because Norah had already pressed her lips to his. His hand tightened on her back, and she sighed. It was everything she had hoped for—and it was more than worth the wait.

She moved to pull back, but he pressed her to him again, and Norah laughed against Stuart's lips. She closed her eyes and lost herself in him. When he deepened the kiss, she lost all sense of who she was or where they were. There was only Stuart, and she didn't want it any other way.

When they both finally parted to catch their breaths, Norah rested her cheek against his chest. He held her close, and she could feel his chest rise and fall.

Nothing could be more perfect than this—to feel so complete with one person.

She closed her eyes and breathed in his scent as she imagined their future together. There was so much to come, and whatever life handed them, she knew that together, she and Stuart would relish the good and come together to work through the bad.

As long as they were together, all would be well.

# Epilogue

*A FEW MONTHS LATER . . .*

With one last push, the settee slid into its new spot near the back wall of the parlor. Norah stepped back and brushed her hands together.

*That* was much better. Now she only needed to rearrange the trinkets and photographs on the mantel, and the parlor would look just as she'd pictured it in her mind.

The front door opened, and Stuart stepped inside. He blinked at the rearranged furniture. "Did you change it again?"

"Yes. I think it's much better this way. See, the settee faces the fireplace, and the two chairs your parents gave us look nice gathered around that little table. What do you think?" She turned an expectant gaze on him.

"I love it," he said immediately.

It was such a quick response that Norah knew he'd never have told her otherwise. She grinned at him. "You can tell me if you dislike it."

"Honestly? I don't have much of an opinion on the arrangement of furniture, so long as I'm not tripping over it." He hung his hat on a peg near the door, and slipped off his coat. "I believe it may actually snow tonight."

Norah clasped her hands together. "Can you imagine curling up here on this settee and watching the snow drift down outside the window?"

Stuart crossed the room and took her in his arms. "I'm glad you're happy with this house."

"It's perfect," Norah replied, wrapping her arms around his waist. The home was small, but it suited them well. It sat near the edge of town, far away from the prison, but was still only a few minutes' walk to reach their friends and families. "Jeremy looked rather wistful about it when he visited earlier. I suspect it won't be long before he leaves Mama and Papa's to find his own home."

"That may happen sooner rather than later, now that our mothers have joined together to find him a wife." Stuart gave a mock shudder, and Norah laughed.

"Ruthann came by with Caleb too. I suspect she'll be asking Nate to find them a house with more room once Caleb begins moving around. She said that apartment over the studio was much too small for a growing family."

"*This* house will be too small for a growing family soon enough," Stuart said.

"Oh? Are you planning for our family to grow larger?" Norah teased.

"I admit little Caleb is quite adorable," Stuart said. "I believe it might be nice to have a baby or two around."

"You know that babies wake up multiple times during the night?" Norah bit her lip to keep from grinning.

"That doesn't last too long, does it?"

"And they have a tendency to spit their meals onto your clothing."

A quick grimace crossed Stuart's face. "Again, that wouldn't last long."

"Our mothers will visit *all* the time."

Stuart laughed. "Are you trying to talk me out of wanting children with you?"

"Not at all," Norah said innocently. "I only needed to ascertain whether you were prepared." She paused a moment and looked up into his eyes, which sparkled with joy at her teasing. "There is nothing I want more than to have a family with you."

And with that, he lowered his head until his lips met hers. Norah closed her eyes, holding onto him as everything around them disappeared. There was only her and Stuart, together. She could stand here, kissing him all night, and not realize that time had passed at all.

But a knock on the door came all too soon, and Stuart pulled away. "Are you expecting someone?"

Norah smiled. "Our mothers. They were wanting to see how I've rearranged the parlor. And I'm certain they'll wish to update us on their new possible matches for Jeremy."

Stuart groaned. "Is it too late for me to return to the office?"

"Yes, and now please let them in."

He did just that, and Mama and Mrs. Joliet burst into the room in a frenzy of coats and hats and hugs. They admired the room, and then Mrs. Joliet launched into asking Stuart about all the unmarried ladies he'd gone to school with.

He shot her a glance, and Norah covered her smile with her hand. She knew he didn't necessarily mind, not after everything they'd almost lost just a few months ago.

She took his hand and smiled at him as he tried to tell his mother that Catherine Rader was not, in fact, widowed, and that her husband was alive and well.

The chatter and good-natured questions fell around Norah like a cozy quilt. It was so good to have family visit in their home.

And, if all went well, it wouldn't be too long before they had new family to fill all of the rooms—and their hearts.

THANK YOU SO MUCH FOR reading! I hope you enjoyed Norah and Stuart's story. There's another book coming in the Brides of Fremont County series. Charlotte never meant to fall in love with the man hired to protect her . . . Look for Charlotte and Mark's story in *Charlotte*[1], coming soon!

Want to read more of my sweet historical western books? A good place to start is with *Building Forever*[2], the first book in my Gilbert Girls series. This series is where you'll find out how Cañon City's Sheriff Ben Young and his wife Penny first met.

To be alerted about my new books, sign up here: http://bit.ly/catsnewsletter I give subscribers a free download of *Forbidden Forever*, a prequel novella to my Gilbert Girls series. You'll also get sneak peeks at upcoming books, insights into the writer life, discounts and deals, inspirations, and so much more. I'd love to have *you* join the fun!

Turn the page to see a complete list of my books, including all the books in the Brides of Fremont County series.

---

1. *https://amzn.to/3ArRtgD*

2.     *http://bit.ly/BuildingForeverbook*

# More Books by Cat Cahill

*Crest Stone Mail-Order Brides* series
A Hopeful Bride[1]
A Rancher's Bride[2]
A Bartered Bride[3]
A Sheriff's Bride[4]
*The Gilbert Girls* series
Building Forever[5]
Running From Forever[6]
Wild Forever[7]
Hidden Forever[8]
Forever Christmas[9]
On the Edge of Forever[10]
The Gilbert Girls Book Collection – Books 1-3[11]

---

1. https://bit.ly/HopefulBride

2. http://bit.ly/RanchersBride

3. https://bit.ly/barteredbride

4. https://amzn.to/3z0PWPr

5. http://bit.ly/BuildingForeverbook

6. http://bit.ly/RunningForeverBook

7. http://bit.ly/WildForeverBook

8. http://bit.ly/HiddenForeverBook

9. http://bit.ly/ForeverChristmasBook

10. http://bit.ly/EdgeofForever

The Gilbert Girls Book Collection – Books 4-6[12]
*Brides of Fremont County* series
Grace[13]
Molly[14]
Ruthann[15]
Norah[16]
Charlotte[17]
**Other Sweet Historical Western Romances by Cat**
*The Proxy Brides* series
A Bride for Isaac [18]
A Bride for Andrew [19]
A Bride for Weston[20]
*The Blizzard Brides* series
A Groom for Celia [21]
A Groom for Faith[22]
A Groom for Josie[23]
*Last Chance Brides* series

11. http://bit.ly/GilbertGirlsBox

12. https://amzn.to/3gYPXcA

13. http://bit.ly/ConfusedColorado

14. https://bit.ly/DejectedDenver

15. https://bit.ly/brideruthann

16. https://amzn.to/3IyJRuA

17. https://amzn.to/3ArRtgD

18. http://bit.ly/BrideforIsaac

19. https://bit.ly/BrideforAndrew

20. https://bit.ly/BrideforWeston

21. http://bit.ly/GroomforCelia

22. http://bit.ly/GroomforFaith

23. https://bit.ly/GroomforJosie

A Chance for Lara[24]
A Chance for Belle[25]
*The Matchmaker's Ball* series
Waltzing with Willa[26]
*Westward Home and Hearts Mail-Order Brides* series
Rose's Rescue[27]
Hazel's Hope[28]
*Matchmaker's Mix-Up* series
William's Wistful Bride[29]
Ransom's Rowdy Bride[30]
*The Sheriff's Mail-Order Bride* series
A Bride for Hawk[31]
*Keepers of the Light* series
The Outlaw's Promise[32]
*Mail-Order Brides' First Christmas* series
A Christmas Carol for Catherine[33]
*The Broad Street Boarding House* series
Starla's Search[34]

---

24. https://amzn.to/3sAj0IV

25. https://amzn.to/3bYgQ1t

26. https://bit.ly/WaltzingwithWilla

27. https://bit.ly/RoseRescue

28. https://amzn.to/3o3P71P

29. https://bit.ly/WilliamsWistfulBride

30. https://amzn.to/3s0Lqwq

31. https://bit.ly/BrideforHawk

32. https://bit.ly/OutlawsPromise

33. https://bit.ly/ChristmasCarolCatherine

34. https://amzn.to/32sQuPS

# About the Author, Cat Cahill

A SUNSET. SNOW ON THE mountains. A roaring river in the spring. A man and a woman who can't fight the love that pulls them together. The danger and uncertainty of life in the Old West. This is what inspires me to write. I hope you find an escape in my books!

I live with my family and a houseful of dogs and cats in Kentucky. When I'm not writing, I'm losing myself in a good book, planning my next travel adventure, doing a puzzle, attempting to garden, or wrangling my kids.

Made in United States
Troutdale, OR
08/05/2023

11837661R00087